Would Annie Come To Him?

Though Jase's body thrummed with need and had since leaving her, he hoped she wouldn't. He feared he wouldn't be able to resist her.

With those laughing green eyes and that sassy mouth, she'd teased him into remembering the pleasures a man could share with a woman. Bewitched him into forgetting the hurt that was inevitable if he allowed anyone to get too close. For the length of an afternoon he'd let go of the memories, the fears.

He heard the door open softly and tensed, knowing it was Annie. Her scent reached him first, that subtle, feminine fragrance that teased his senses.

"Jase?"

He prayed for the strength to send her back to her room. But when he looked at her, he knew the prayer was wasted.

There was no way in hell he could send her away. Not now.

Dear Reader,

Welcome to Silhouette Desire, the ultimate treat for Valentine's Day—we promise you will find six passionate, powerful and provocative romances every month! And here's what you can indulge yourself with this February....

The fabulous Peggy Moreland brings you February's MAN OF THE MONTH, *The Way to a Rancher's Heart*. You'll be enticed by this gruff widowed rancher who must let down his guard for the sake of a younger woman.

The exciting Desire miniseries TEXAS CATTLEMAN'S CLUB: LONE STAR JEWELS continues with *World's Most Eligible Texan* by Sara Orwig. A world-weary diplomat finds love—and fatherhood—after making a Plain Jane schoolteacher pregnant with his child.

Kathryn Jensen's *The American Earl* is an office romance featuring the son of a British earl who falls for his American employee. In *Overnight Cinderella* by Katherine Garbera, an ugly-duckling heroine transforms herself into a swan to win the love of an alpha male. Kate Little tells the story of a wealthy bachelor captivated by the woman he was trying to protect his younger brother from in *The Millionaire Takes a Bride*. And Kristi Gold offers *His Sheltering Arms*, in which a macho ex-cop finds love with the woman he protects.

Make this Valentine's Day extra-special by spoiling yourself with all six of these alluring Desire titles!

Enjoy!

Joan Marlow Golan

Joan Marlow Golan
Senior Editor, Silhouette Desire

Please address questions and book requests to:
Silhouette Reader Service
U.S.: 3010 Walden Ave., P.O. Box 1325, Buffalo, NY 14269
Canadian: P.O. Box 609, Fort Erie, Ont. L2A 5X3

The Way to a Rancher's Heart

PEGGY MORELAND

Silhouette® Desire®

Published by Silhouette Books

America's Publisher of Contemporary Romance

SILHOUETTE BOOKS

ISBN 0-373-76345-X

THE WAY TO A RANCHER'S HEART

Copyright © 2001 by Peggy Bozeman Morse

This edition published by arrangement with Harlequin Books S.A.

® and TM are trademarks of Harlequin Books S.A., used under license. Trademarks indicated with ® are registered in the United States Patent and Trademark Office, the Canadian Trade Marks Office and in other countries.

Visit Silhouette at www.eHarlequin.com

Printed in U.S.A.

PEGGY MORELAND

published her first romance with Silhouette in 1989 and continues to delight readers with stories set in her home state of Texas. Winner of the National Readers' Choice Award, the Golden Quill, the Texas Gold and a finalist for the prestigious RITA Award, Peggy's books frequently appear on the *USA Today* and Waldenbooks bestseller lists. When not writing, she enjoys spending time at the farm riding her quarter horse, Lo-Jump. She, her husband and three children make their home in Florence, Texas. You may write to Peggy at P.O. Box 1099, Florence, TX 76257-1099.

This book is dedicated to my editor, Lynda Curnyn,
with heartfelt thanks for all the guidance and support
offered to me...and my apologies for forcing her
to learn a new language, Texas-ese. Thanks, Lynda!

One

There was tired, then there was *tired,* the boot-shuffling, butt-dragging, bleary-eyed kind of exhaustion that followed too many nights without enough sleep and too many days filled with nonstop activity. Jase Rawley's current physical state fell into that latter category.

After parking his semi-rig and trailer filled with stocker calves he'd hauled from Kansas to Texas beside the loading chute attached to his corral, he trudged wearily through the inky darkness to his equally dark house in the distance. Once inside, he toed off his cowboy boots by the kitchen door, left them there for easy access the next morning, then tugged his shirttail from the waist of his jeans and headed down the hall to the master bedroom, unbuttoning his shirt along the way. At the side of his bed, he stripped off the shirt, leaned to set the alarm on the bedside table for 6:00 a.m., then, all but limp with exhaustion, fell face-first across the king-size bed. He was instantly asleep.

Three hours later he awakened to the irritating electronic beep of his alarm clock. Groaning, he made a fist, whacked it against the alarm, then buried his face against the mattress again. He inhaled deeply, wearily, weighing the pros and cons of putting off unloading the calves for a few more hours. But the rich, nutty smell of coffee brewing had him slowly lifting his head again.

Bracing his palms against the mattress, he lifted himself higher, sniffing the air. ''Sis,'' he murmured almost reverently as he heaved himself from the bed and to his feet, ''you're a saint.''

With his nose lifted high like a radar device, guiding him to the coffeepot, he padded his way down the hallway, still dressed in the jeans and socks he'd slept in. A yawn took him as he stepped into the kitchen, and he closed his eyes, giving in to it, as he passed by the island, rubbing a wide hand over his burly chest. ''Mornin','' he grumbled as he drew a bead on the coffeemaker and headed for it.

''Good morning. Would you like your eggs fried or scrambled?''

He froze at the question, then slowly turned, focusing in on the woman who stood on the opposite side of the island calmly rolling out biscuits. Above a pert nose sprinkled with a light spattering of freckles, bright, cheery green eyes met his, while full lips curved upwards in a not-normal-for-this-time-of-morning smile. Brown hair, the color of roasted chestnuts, spilled over slim shoulders and framed an oval, youthful face...a face that looked nothing like his sister's.

"Who the hell are you?" he asked in dismay.

Her smile widened and she wiped a palm across the bib of her apron as she rounded the island. "Annie Baxter," she said and held out the hand, now free of flour. "I'm your new housekeeper and nanny."

He stared at the flour streaks her hand had left on the apron's bib, the T-shirt and cut-off jeans the apron didn't quite hide, then moved his gaze farther down to the length of long, tanned legs beneath the apron's hem, the bare feet, the toenails painted a putrid shade of blue. Slowly he lifted his gaze back to hers, without making a move to accept the hand she offered. "Housekeeper?" he repeated dully.

Her smile turned curious. "Well, yes. Your sister hired me. Penny Rawley?" she offered helpfully, as if hearing his sister's name might prod his memory. "You were aware that she planned to hire someone, weren't you?"

He gulped, then swallowed, remembering, vaguely, a conversation with his sister a couple of weeks earlier in which she'd told him she was moving out. He seemed, too, to remember her saying something about hiring someone to take her place in his home. But he hadn't taken his sister seriously. Had thought she was bluffing. She had more than once over the years. Penny had *always* lived with him. Had ever since their parents had died more than fifteen years before. He hadn't thought she'd really leave. Ever. Hadn't even considered the possibility. Penny was a fixture, a solid rock of dependability that he'd relied on heavily since his wife's death two years before.

"Yeah," he said and swallowed again. "I seem to remember her mentioning something about that." Realizing she still held her hand extended, he closed his fingers around hers and slowly pumped her hand.

"Whew," she said, laughing softly. "That's a relief. I thought, for a minute, that either you or I were in the wrong house." She withdrew her hand to move back to the opposite side of the island. "Penny told me that you'd be returning today, although I didn't realize it would be quite this early."

"I decided to drive straight through," he murmured, still having a hard time absorbing the fact that Penny was gone and had left a stranger in her place. "How long have you been here?"

"Six days. Penny hired me on Monday, stayed until Thursday to make sure I had settled in well and the children had accepted me, then she left."

And Jase knew why his sister had cleared out before he'd returned from his trip. If he'd been home, he never would have allowed her to take the first step out the front door...at least not without him first putting up one hell of a fight. "Did she say where she was going? How she could be reached?"

"Well, of course she did," she replied, as if surprised by his question, then wiped her hands across her apron again and turned to the desk behind her. Snagging a pad between the tips of a flour-dusted finger and thumb, she turned and held it out to him. "She said that she was staying with Suzy for a couple of days. You do know who Suzy is, don't you?"

He frowned at her skeptical tone, though he could

hardly blame her for questioning him. Not when he hadn't even known that his sister was planning on moving out or that she was hiring him a new house-keeper and nanny. "Yeah," he grumbled. "I know Suzy." Tearing off the top piece of paper, he stuffed it into his jeans pocket, then tossed the pad on the island before heading for the coffeemaker.

"You never did say how you liked your eggs," she reminded him, dropping plump rounds of dough into a pie tin. "Fried or scrambled?"

He filled a mug with coffee and turned, gulping a swallow, praying that the caffeine would clear his brain, and he'd realize that this was all a bad dream. Something he'd imagined. Hell, a full-blown night-mare!

But when the strange woman didn't disappear in a cloud of mist as he'd hoped, but kept right on cutting dough into rounds and dropping them into the pie tin, he muttered, "fried," and headed for the door that led to the hallway. "I've got to make a few calls," he called over his shoulder. "Holler when breakfast is ready."

The first—and only—call Jase made was to Suzy's house and to his sister.

He waited impatiently through four rings before his sister's childhood friend answered.

"Hello?" Suzy mumbled sleepily.

"Put Penny on the phone," he growled.

"Well, good morning to you, too, Jase," she snapped peevishly, then dropped the phone with a clatter and yelled, "Penny! Phone! It's the bear."

Scowling at the nickname Suzy had tagged him

with years before, he drummed his fingers impatiently on the top of his desk while he waited for his sister to pick up the phone.

"Jase?"

"What the hell were you thinking!" he shouted as soon as he heard her voice. "Running off and leaving these kids with a complete stranger."

"Annie's not a stranger," she said defensively, then added, "Well, not totally, anyway. I interviewed her thoroughly and checked her background and references before offering her the position. She's perfectly safe and more than capable of taking care of the children."

"I don't give a good goddamn if she's Mary Poppins's trainer. You get your tail back home where you belong, and I mean *now!*"

"I'm not coming home, Jase. I've already accepted a job in Austin."

"You've *what!*"

"I've accepted a job in Austin. Quite a good one, in fact. I'll be the executive secretary to the owner of a large computer security company."

"Quit," he said, tossing up an angry hand. "Resign. Do whatever you have to do, but you get yourself back here where you belong. I don't want some stranger raising my kids."

"Then *you* raise them!"

Jase jerked the receiver from his ear and stared at it, shocked by the anger in his sister's voice, and even more so that she would defy him. Scowling, he slapped the phone back against his ear. "Is Suzy behind all this? Is she the one who put these crazy ideas into your head?"

A heavy sigh crossed the phone lines. "No, Jase. Suzy had nothing to do with my decision to leave the ranch."

"Oh, that's right, Jase," he heard Suzy mutter in the background. "Blame everything on me."

"Well, she's usually the one who fills your head with these crazy notions," he snapped irritably. "This isn't like you, Penny. Running off half-cocked. Leaving the kids with a complete stranger. Hell! What if this woman doesn't work out? What if she decides to up and leave? Who's going to take care of the kids then?"

"You," she informed him firmly. "They're *your* children, not mine, and it's high time you pulled yourself together and assumed your responsibilities as their father."

He sprang from his chair. "I've never shirked my responsibilities as their father! I've provided for these kids, haven't I? I've seen that they have everything they need."

"You give them everything but yourself. Oh, Jase," she said, suddenly sounding tearful. "They need you. Can't you see that? They not only lost their mother when Claire died, they lost their father, too."

After showering and dressing, Jase returned to the kitchen, still furious with his sister for abandoning him and sticking a stranger in his house without discussing it with him first. He heard the sound of his six-year-old daughter's laughter from the hallway as he pushed open the swinging door. "What's so funny?" he asked, pausing with a hand still braced against the door.

Four heads turned from the table to peer at him.

In the blink of an eye, Rachel was up and racing across the room to throw her arms around his waist. "Daddy!"

He dropped an awkward hand on her head and scrubbed, frowning. "Hey, dumplin'."

She caught his hand and gave it a tug. "We've got a new nanny. Annie. She's really cool."

His frown deepened at the term Rachel used to describe the new nanny, suspecting that she had picked it up from her older brother and sister. "Yeah. So I hear."

He clapped a hand on his thirteen-year-old son Clay's shoulder, then dropped down onto the chair at the head of the table. He nodded a greeting to Clay's twin sister, Tara, and pulled his napkin from beside his plate. He draped it across his thigh while carefully avoiding making eye contact with the new nanny. "Shouldn't you kids be getting ready for school?" he asked gruffly.

Tara rolled her eyes dramatically, her newest way of expressing what a "dweeb" she thought her father was. "It's not even seven yet, Dad. We've got lots of time."

Jase reached for the basket of biscuits. "Don't want you missing the bus," he informed her. "I've got a trailer full of calves to unload and don't have time to cart you kids' butts to school."

Tara tossed her napkin down and shoved back her chair. "Since when do you have time to do anything with us?" she snapped and stormed from the room.

Jase watched her leave, noting the hiking boots, the low-waisted, baggy-legged, faded jeans and the inch of bare skin her cropped T-shirt exposed. "Change into something decent!" he yelled after her. "No daughter of mine is going to school dressed like some tramp."

He heard her sass something in return, but couldn't make out her words. Scowling, he spread a heavy layer of butter over his biscuit and remembered his sister's comments about him assuming responsibility for his kids. Well, he *was* responsible, he told himself. He had let go of a lot of things over the last couple of years, but he'd never let go of his responsibilities to his kids. To prove it, he asked, "Did you kids do all your homework?"

"Yes, Daddy," Rachel said obediently.

As he took a bite, he angled his head to look at Clay, who had remained conspicuously silent. Butter dripped down his chin, as he gave it a jerk in his son's direction. "What about you? Did you get yours done?"

Clay shoved back his chair. "Didn't have any," he mumbled and headed for the door and the hallway beyond.

Jase snatched up his napkin and wiped it across his mouth and chin. "I better not be getting any calls from your teachers," he called after his son. He shifted his gaze to Rachel, who remained at the table, staring at him, round-eyed. "Well? Are you planning on going to school today, or not?"

"I'm goin'," she replied quickly and slid from her chair. "Thanks for breakfast, Annie," she said, giving the new nanny a shy smile. "It was real good."

Annie graced her with a radiant smile in return.

"I'm glad you enjoyed it. Don't forget your lunch," she reminded the girl.

Rachel sidled to the side of Annie's chair, winding a finger through a pigtail. "Did you pack me a surprise like you did on Friday?"

Annie draped an arm around Rachel's waist and hugged her to her side. "You bet I did. But don't peek," she warned, tapping a finger against the end of the child's nose. "It won't be a surprise if you do."

A pleased smile spread across Rachel's face. "I won't," she promised and skipped to the counter to collect her lunch sack. "See you this afternoon, Annie," she called cheerfully as she raced for the back door.

"Not if I see you first," Annie teased, waving.

Jase frowned, more than a little surprised by his children's obvious approval of the new nanny—and maybe a little jealous, if he were willing to admit to the emotion. And now, with all the kids gone, only he and the nanny remained at the table and he wished he hadn't been so quick to hustle them off to school. Uncomfortable with the silence that suddenly seemed to hum around him, he cleared his throat. "I guess Penny informed you of your duties."

"Yes. She was very thorough."

Unsure what else to say, he quickly slathered butter over another biscuit. "I'm outside most of the day, but if you should need anything, I have a cell phone in my truck. The number is on the wall by the phone," he added, gesturing with the biscuit toward the wall.

"Penny explained everyone's schedules to me and

showed me where to find everything.'' She propped her elbows on the table and leaned forward, studying him, her chin resting on her hands. ''The children miss you when you're gone.''

Feeling heat creep into his cheeks, Jase shoveled a forkful of eggs into his mouth. ''I'm seldom away. When I am, it's never for more than a week at a time.''

''Just the same, they miss their daddy.''

He cleared his throat again and reached for his cup, gulped a drink of coffee, then shoved back his chair. ''I've got calves to unload.''

She kept her gaze on his face as he rose. ''Do you plan to come in for lunch?''

He was tempted to tell her no, just to avoid being alone with her again, but thought better of it. It was a helluva long time until dinner. ''Yeah. But you don't have to cook. I can make a sandwich or something.''

She rose, too, and started gathering plates. ''I don't mind cooking. In fact, I really enjoy it. Is there anything special you'd like me to prepare?''

Jase snagged his hat from the countertop where he'd dropped it the night before and glanced her way as she headed for the sink, juggling dirty plates. He couldn't help noticing that the bibbed apron she wore didn't cover her rear end or hide the sway of a very delectably shaped butt. He cleared his throat yet again when his gaze lit on her bare feet, and heat climbed up his neck, burning his cheeks. ''I'm not a picky eater,'' he mumbled and tore his gaze away from what shouldn't have been a erotic sight. ''Whatever you put on the table is fine with me.''

She glanced over her shoulder and warmed his face even more with a smile. "Good. I'll surprise you, then. Should I expect you about noon?"

Flustered, he rammed his hat over his head and turned for the back door. "Yeah, noon," he muttered, and wondered if the surprise she had in store for him was anything like the one she'd secreted in his daughter's school lunch.

Annie strolled through the small fenced area, studying the ground and the barely discernable rows that lay beneath the high weeds, enjoying the feel of the sun warming her skin. A garden, she thought dreamily. She could imagine rows of tomato plants, their branches sagging with fat, juicy tomatoes; cantaloupe vines crawling across freshly hoed rows, their plump, succulent rounds of yellow- and green-veined rinds peeking between the plants' velvety, scalloped leaves.

Oh, how she'd love to plant a garden, she thought, sighing wistfully. It had been years since she'd worked a garden, dug her fingers in rich, fertile soil, feasted on a garden's bounty. Four years to be exact. The summer before her grandmother passed away.

With another sigh, one filled with bittersweet memories this time, she walked on, deciding she might just ask her new boss for permission to clear out the weeds and plant a few vegetables. There was time yet before spring arrived fully.

She frowned as she thought of her new boss. Penny Rawley certainly hadn't exaggerated when she'd said that her brother was a little reserved, perhaps might even appear a bit gruff. Gruff? She snorted at the mild description. The man was positively sour. Frowning all the time. All but growling at his children.

But, my, oh my, she thought with a lusty sigh, he was one prime hunk of man.

She shivered just thinking about the way he'd looked when he'd walked into the kitchen that morning, his eyelids still heavy with sleep, rubbing a wide hand over the soft mat of dark hair that swirled over a muscled chest. She wondered if he realized that the first button of his jeans had been unfastened. She wondered, too, if he realized how sexy she had found that glimpse of navel shadowed by dark hair, the equally dark V that seemed to point below the waist of his jeans and to the soft column of flesh that lay beneath a strip of fabric faded a slightly lighter shade than the rest of the denim.

With a delicious shiver, she leaned to pluck a bachelor's button from the tangled weeds and straightened to tuck the bloom behind her ear.

"What are you doing?"

She jumped, startled, and turned to find her new employer standing behind her watching her, his arms folded across his chest, his hat shading his eyes. She huffed a breath. "Mercy! You might warn a person before you slip up on them unsuspecting. You scared a good ten years off my life!"

He narrowed an eye. "How old are you, anyway?"

She snatched the flower from behind her ear, sure that it was her foolishness that made him question her age. "Twenty-six."

He snorted a disbelieving breath. "Try again."

Mindful of the stickers that might be hiding beneath the tangle of weeds, she made her way carefully back to the gate. "I *am* twenty-six. If you don't believe me, I can show you my driver's license." She reached the gate and opened it.

He stepped back, eyeing her suspiciously as she passed by. "You don't look a day over eighteen."

She chuckled, not sure whether to be pleased or insulted. "Thanks...I think." Flipping her hair back over her shoulder, she tipped up her face to smile at him, having to squint against the glare of the sun to do so. "How old are you?"

He stared down at her a long moment, making her aware of the skimpy tank top she wore, the Daisy Duke cutoffs, her bare legs and feet. Then he dropped his arms from his chest, stuffed his hands into the pockets of his jeans and turned for the house. "Old enough to stay clear of young girls like you."

She sputtered a laugh. "Young girls like me?" she repeated, following him. "And what is that supposed to mean?"

He lifted a shoulder as he opened the screen door, then stepped back to let her enter the house first. "When I was younger, we called 'em jailbait. But I guess now I'd just call 'em trouble."

"Trouble?" When he didn't offer an explanation, she stopped in front of him, folding her arms beneath her breasts and arching a brow, stubbornly refusing to enter until he had clarified that last comment. His gaze dropped to her chest and breasts that strained against her tank top's fabric. She bit back a smile as a blush rose to stain his cheeks.

"*Trouble,*" he repeated, emphasizing the single word, as if it alone explained everything, then gave her a nudge with his shoulder, urging her through the door ahead of him.

"Okay," she said and crossed to the sink to wash her hands. "Granted I'm younger than you. Even I can see that. But what's wrong with a young woman, and why do you consider one trouble?"

"Woman?" He snorted at her choice of word. "I said *girl*. I would hardly classify you as a woman."

She snagged a dish towel from the hook above the sink and dried her hands as she turned to peer at him. "And what does a *girl* have to do," she asked, placing emphasis on the word as he had, "in your opinion, before she is classified as a woman?"

He elbowed her aside and hit the faucet's handle, then stuck his hands beneath the water. "Live. Get some years on her. Some experience."

Enjoying the conversation, but unsure why when she knew she should be insulted by his chauvinistic attitude, she rested a hip against the counter and watched as he scrubbed his hands. "And what do you consider experience?"

He scowled and hit the handle with his wrist, shutting off the water. He stood, dripping water into the sink, and Annie pushed the towel into his hands. He shot her a look, his scowl deepening. "Live," he repeated. "Life offers its own form of experience."

She angled her body, watching as he crossed to the refrigerator. "Oh, really?" she posed dryly.

"Yeah, really," he muttered, his reply muffled by the interior of the refrigerator. He pulled a gallon jug of milk from inside, closed the door, then lifted the jug, drinking directly from the container.

Clucking her tongue at his lack of manners, Annie

pulled a glass from the cupboard, crossed to him and snatched the milk jug from his hand.

Scowling, he wiped the back of his hand across his mouth, removing a white moustache. "What did you do that for? I'm thirsty."

She filled the glass and handed it back to him. "Unsanitary," she informed him prudently and opened the door to replace the jug of milk. "And a bad example for the children. Now I know where Clay picked up the habit." She pulled out a bowl and crossed to the table. "I hope you like pasta, because that's what I made for lunch."

Still frowning, he followed her to the table and sat down in his chair at the head of it, eyeing the bowl's contents with distrust. "What's in it?"

"Pasta curls, grilled vegetables, some herbs, a little olive oil and balsamic vinegar."

He reared back, curling his nose and eyeing the bowl warily. "I'm a meat and potatoes man, myself."

"Really?" she asked, nonplused, and sat down in the chair at his right. "I'd think after working around those smelly old calves all morning that you'd have lost your taste for beef."

He jerked his head up to glare at her. "I'll have you know those smelly old calves help pay the bills around here."

She lifted a shoulder and spooned a generous serving of pasta onto his plate. "If you don't eat the merchandise, then that just means more profit, right?"

His thick brows drew together over his nose. "What the hell kind of thinking is that?"

She lifted a shoulder as she served her own plate. "Rational. The less you eat, the more beef you have to sell." She lifted her shoulder again as she set the bowl back on the table. "Makes sense to me."

He huffed a breath and picked up his fork, shaking his head. "Yeah. I guess to a *girl* like you, that would make sense."

Heaving a long-suffering sigh, she turned to look at him. "Are we back to that topic again?"

He scooped up a forkful of pasta and shoveled it into his mouth. "Yeah, I guess we are."

Stretching across the table for the breadbasket, she tore off a section of the still-warm loaf and dropped it onto his plate before tearing off a piece for herself. "If that's all you can think to talk about, your conversational skills are lacking. You really should work on that."

"Nothing wrong with my conversational skills," he informed her and lifted his fork for another bite. "You're just pissed because I called you a *girl*."

She shook her head and sank back in her chair, watching him wolf down the pasta. And he'd said he was a meat and potatoes man, she thought, biting back a smile. "I'm not insulted because you referred to me as a girl. I am a girl. A female. And proud of it. But I *am* a bit surprised that you'd make an assumption on my level of experience, based on your definition of the term," she added pointedly, "considering you know absolutely nothing about me."

He cocked his head to peer at her, then waved his fork in her direction before returning his attention to his meal. "Okay. I'll bite. Tell me about yourself."

She reached for her glass of water and took a sip, then propped her elbows on the table, cradling the glass between her hands. "I'm a graduate of the University of Texas where I majored in art and minored in secondary education. I obtained my master's degree in December.''

He lifted an eyebrow, obviously impressed. ''A college graduate, huh? So what's a woman with that much education doing working as a housekeeper and nanny?''

It was her turn to lift an indifferent shoulder. ''I like to eat. When you graduate in December, teaching jobs are a little hard to come by.''

''You plan to teach?''

''Yes, and I hope to do some freelancing on the side.''

''What kind of freelancing?''

''Photography. I plan to supplement my income by selling photos, and possibly accompanying articles, to magazines and journals.''

''Sounds like you've got your future all planned out nice and tidy.''

''Yes,'' she agreed, but was unable to resist the urge to dig at him a little. ''So does that make me mature, more experienced? By your definition, a woman, rather than a *girl?*''

He snorted and laid down his fork, then reared back in his chair and leveled his gaze on her. ''Experience comes with knocks. The hard kind. That's where I got my degree. The school of hard knocks.''

''And what kind of knocks have you had in your life?''

His gray eyes, once intent upon hers and filled with something akin to humor, took on a hooded look, as if a black cloud had swept across them, hiding his emotions. He rose and carried his glass to the sink to rinse it out and refill it with water, then stood, staring out the window.

"My parents died in a car wreck when I was nineteen," he said after a moment, his voice roughened by the memories. "I was a freshman at Texas A&M. Had to come home and take over the ranch. My sister, Penny, was thirteen. The courts appointed me her legal guardian." He stood a moment longer, staring out the window, then angled his head to narrow an eye at her. "My wife died two years ago. Brain aneurysm. Gone like that," he said, with a snap of his fingers. "Without any warning. Left me with three kids under the age of eleven to raise on my own."

"You had Penny," she reminded him, fighting back the swell of sympathy that rose.

Scowling, he turned to face the window again. "*Had* being the operative word."

"You still have her," she insisted. "Just because she chose to pursue her own life doesn't mean that she's extracted herself permanently from yours."

He shot her a glare over his shoulder. "Sure you didn't get that degree in psychology?"

She shook her head. "No. Art. But I'm a people watcher. It's a hobby of mine. And do you know what I see when I look at you?"

"What?" he asked drolly.

"A man who feels sorry for himself."

He slammed the glass down on the counter so hard that water shot above the lip like a geyser. He spun to face her, his face flushed with anger. "I don't feel sorry for myself. I've taken the cards I've been dealt and played them as best I could. Nobody can question that. Least of all *you.*"

She rose and crossed to him. "Maybe I don't have the right, but I *do* think I'm correct in assuming you feel sorry for yourself. And now you're blaming your sister for leaving you to take care of your children alone."

He grabbed her by the shoulders, his eyes boring into hers as he glowered down at her. "You listen to me little *girl*," he grated out through clenched teeth. "I don't blame Penny for anything, other than taking off without giving me any warning."

Undaunted by his anger, by the dig of his fingers into her flesh, she met his gaze squarely, maybe a bit stubbornly. "She warned you she was leaving. You told me so yourself just this morning."

He continued to glower at her, a muscle ticking on his jaw, then he released her, pushing her away from him as he turned back to face the window. "I didn't believe her. She'd said before she was going to leave, but she never went through with it."

"And you're angry with her because this time she did what she said she was going to do."

He whirled to face her, his gray eyes hard as steel. "The kids need her. They depend upon her. And she walked out on them."

"They need *you*," she argued. "Their father."

He thrust his face close to hers. "And what makes you an authority on what a kid needs? Huh? What the hell makes you think you know better than I do what my own kids need?"

She drew in a long breath, never once moving her gaze from his. "Because I was a kid once myself. My father died of a heart attack when I was five. My mother never got over the loss. She committed suicide when I was six. I *needed* my father,'' she said, and blinked back the unexpected tears that rose. ''And I needed my mother, too. But she wimped out. Left me all alone.'' She hitched a breath but refused to let the tears fall. ''That's how I know,'' she said, her voice growing as steely as the eyes that met hers. ''You want to talk about hard knocks?'' She tapped a finger against his chest. ''Mister, I'll compare lumps with you any day of the week.''

Two

Annie experienced a brief stab of remorse for the sharp words she'd exchanged with her employer...but, thankfully, it didn't last long. She dispensed with it by assuring herself that he'd deserved the tongue-lashing she'd given him.

Calling her a *girl,* she reflected irritably as she stripped the sheets from the children's beds. And carrying on as if he were the only person in the world who had suffered any losses. Well, she had suffered her share of losses, too. But she had *dealt* with her losses, accepting them as natural occurrences in life, situations totally out of her control, and had gone on living, which was more than she could say for Jase Rawley. Instead of dealing with his grief, it appeared he had dug himself a hole and climbed inside where he continued to lick his wounds, shutting out his children and anyone else who tried to get too close.

But his children needed him, she thought, feeling the frustration returning. Couldn't he see that? She certainly could and she'd only been living in his home for a week. Well, he was going to have to climb out of that hole, she told herself as she stuffed the linens into the washing machine. Even if it meant her throwing a stick of dynamite into the hole he'd dug for himself and blasting him out.

Pleased with the image that thought drew, Annie started the first load of laundry, then went to the master bedroom to remove the sheets from Jase's bed. Though she'd been in his room several times during the week, she hadn't entered her employer's private quarters since his late-night return. She noticed immediately the changes his presence made in the room. The sharp, spicy scent of aftershave lingered in the air, as did the faint odor she'd learned to associate with the corral and the livestock herded in and out of it almost daily.

She stooped to pick up a pair of socks from the floor and held her nose, grimacing, as she deposited them in the hamper in the master bath where she noticed more signs of her employer's presence. A wet towel lay on the floor, discarded after his morning shower, she was sure. A toothbrush was angled over the edge of the sink and an assortment of coins were scattered over the tile countertop where he'd obviously emptied his pockets before dropping the jeans to the floor. She nudged a fingertip through the pile of loose change, finding a rusty nail and a crumpled receipt amongst the coins, as well as a tattered package of antacids.

Shaking her head at the odd accumulation, she picked up the jeans and dropped them in the clothes hamper before returning to the bedroom. She frowned slightly as she noticed that the bed, though rumpled, was already made. Had he made it up himself? she wondered, then snorted a laugh when she noticed the imprint of his body on the comforter and realized that he hadn't even bothered to turn down the bed when he'd arrived home, but had opted to sleep on top of the covers instead.

With a rueful shake of her head, she ripped back the comforter and quickly stripped off the sheets. Wadding them into her arms, she headed for the laundry room, but slowed in the hallway, her attention captured by the gallery of framed pictures hanging there. Though she'd looked at the photos before, she found her curiosity heightened after her earlier, heated conversation with her employer.

Pictures of Rachel and the twins dominated the wall, monitoring the children's growth from birth to present day, but Annie found herself skimming over them in search of pictures of Jase. She smiled as she recognized a picture of him with Penny, taken when his sister was probably about Tara's age. Jase stood apart from Penny, yet there was an unmistakable protectiveness in his posture that indicated he took his responsibilities as his sister's guardian very seriously.

Though he was much younger in the picture, Annie noticed that Jase hadn't changed much over the years. In fact, she was sure she recognized the grim scowl and the steely-eyed impatience as the same expression he'd graced her with at breakfast and again at noon.

With a sigh, she shifted her gaze to Penny. Plain, but by no means unattractive, in the photograph Penny projected an image of solemnity unnatural for one so young. Annie supposed it was due to the tragedies Penny had suffered so early in life, the responsibilities she'd been forced to assume.

Though she'd only known Jase's sister a short span of time, Annie suspected she knew Penny better than her own brother did. She attributed that advantage to her fondness for studying people, noting their mannerisms and habits, the little quirks that spoke volumes about their personalities. Too, people tended to tell her things about themselves, guarded little secrets that they wouldn't dream of sharing with another. She wasn't sure why that was so, though she suspected it was simply because she was willing to listen. For whatever reason, throughout her life she had found herself serving as a sounding board and vault for the problems and dreams of countless others, just as she had for Penny in the short week they had spent together before Penny's departure.

Penny Rawley was way past spreading her wings a little, Annie reaffirmed as she moved farther down the hallway. From what Penny had told her, the woman had dedicated herself and her life to Jase and his family. Especially so after the death of Jase's wife.

Reaching a wedding portrait framed in gilt, Annie stopped in front of it, tilting her head slightly as she studied the couple pictured there. So young, she thought with a twinge of sadness as she focused on the bride smiling radiantly and lovingly up at her husband, a bouquet of white roses clutched beneath her chin. And what a scar her passing had left on Jase, she reflected with regret, noting the devotion with which he gazed down upon his wife and remembering the bitterness of his expression when he'd snapped his fingers, demonstrating the quickness of her passing. That he'd loved his wife was obvious in the gesture. That he still harbored resentment, maybe even anger over her loss was even more obvious.

Pensive, she moved on to the laundry room, stuffed the dirty linens into the washing machine, then headed outside with a basket loaded with those she'd already washed. The warmth of the sun and the sound of birds singing in the centuries-old oak tree at the corner of the backyard chased her concerns for Jase and his family from her mind and drew a cheerful smile. Humming an accompaniment to the birds' warbled songs she drew a sheet from the basket, caught it by its corners and clipped it to the clothesline, then reached inside the basket for another.

"We have a clothes dryer."

Annie jumped, then sagged weakly, clutching the damp sheet against her chest as she turned to frown at Jase. "You've got to quit doing that," she scolded.

"Doing what?"

"Sneaking up on me like that."

He lifted a shoulder. "Wasn't sneaking. Was on my way to the house." He gestured to the sheet she still held against her chest. "Thought I ought to let you know we have a clothes dryer and save you the trouble of hanging the sheets on the line."

She huffed a breath as she turned. "I know there's a clothes dryer," she replied, thinking of the mountains of dirty laundry she'd washed since her arrival in his home. She plucked a clothespin from the line and clipped it over the sheet, securing it in place. "I just happen to prefer sun-dried linens."

He lifted an indifferent shoulder. "It's your back."

"Yes, it is," she agreed and squatted down beside the basket to dig through the remaining linens for the matching pillowcases to hang. "And speaking of my back, would you mind if I strained it a little more by cleaning out the garden and planting a few vegetables?"

When he didn't respond immediately, she glanced up and found that he'd turned and was staring at the garden plot, his eyes narrowed, his jaw set in a hard line. Seeing the slow bob of his Adam's apple, she quickly rose. "If you'd rather I didn't—"

He shook his head and walked away. "Do what you want with it," he muttered.

She stared after him, wondering what it was about her request that he found so upsetting.

Still puzzling over Jase's strange reaction to her request to plant a garden, Annie whacked at the weeds choking the small piece of ground. She'd cleared a space about three feet by three feet when the hairs on the back of her neck prickled. Sensing that she was being watched, she glanced up and saw Jase standing in the opening of the barn's loft, shirtless, his hands braced high on the opening's frame. Sweat gleamed on his muscled arms and chest and darkened the waist of his jeans.

Though his hat shadowed his face, she felt the intensity of his gaze, the unmistakable heat in it. As he continued to stare, she drew a hand to the hollow of her throat, suddenly feeling exposed, as if he'd somehow managed to strip her of her clothing and left her standing naked in the garden.

An awareness passed between them, something primitive and sexual that had Annie's pulse pummeling her palm, her mouth going dry as dust. She wanted to look away...but found she couldn't. She could only stare in slack-jawed fascination at the virile image he created standing high in the loft, one knee slightly bent, one hip cocked a little higher than the other. He looked so commanding, so utterly masculine, so bone-meltingly sexual. And when he dropped a hand to rub it lazily across the dark, damp hair on his chest, she closed her eyes, suddenly feeling weak, sure that she could feel the damp heat on her lips, taste on her tongue the salt from his skin.

Anxious for another look, she opened her eyes, but he was already turning away. Stifling the moan of disappointment that rose, the sense of loss, she slowly caught up the hoe and began to chop half-heartedly at the weeds again, her movements sluggish now, her strength drained by the attraction that churned low in her belly.

Her thoughts were so scattered, her senses so dulled, it took a moment for her to become aware of the rumble of the school bus. Straightening, she drew the hoe up, propped her hands on its handle and inhaled a deep, steadying breath, pushing back her lustful thoughts of Jase as she watched the bus near.

It stopped in front of the house and the door folded back. Rachel, always seated at the front of the bus, came tumbling down the steps, dragging her book bag behind her, and headed straight for the house.

"Hey, Rachel!" she called, lifting a hand in greeting. "Over here. How was school?"

A grin spreading from ear to ear, Rachel raced toward the garden, waving a paper above her head. "Annie! Look! I made a hundred on my spelling test!"

"Why, that's wonderful, sweetheart!" Annie stepped from the garden and leaned the hoe against the low fence, then knelt and wrapped an arm around the girl's waist, drawing her to her side. "And look," she said pointing, "your teacher gave you a gold star, too."

"That's 'cause my penmanship was so good."

"And it is," Annie agreed, hugging the girl to her.

"What's for dinner?"

Annie glanced up at the question and saw Tara headed her way, followed closely by Clay. She widened her smile to include the twins. "Dinner isn't for a couple of hours, yet, but there are fresh vegetables in the refrigerator and some dip, if you'd like a snack."

Tara rolled her eyes and did a neat U-turn, heading for the house. "Rabbit food," she muttered under her breath.

Surprised by the teenager's sour expression, Annie rose, staring after her.

"Ignore her," Clay said. "She's in one of her moods."

"It certainly appears that way," Annie replied, wondering if the mood was a carryover from the teenager's brief but heated confrontation with her father that morning. "And how was your day?" she asked, turning to smile at Clay.

"Okay."

"Kiss any girls?" she teased.

He ducked his head, blushing, and chipped the toe of a boot against the ground. "Nah."

Annie laughed. "Well, there's always tomorrow."

He glanced up at her, then quickly away, his blush deepening, then shifted his gaze to the garden. "What are you doing out here?"

"Getting the soil ready to plant." She glanced at the garden and sighed wearily, disappointed by the small amount of progress she'd made. "But it's turning out to be a much bigger chore than I anticipated."

"Does Dad know you're working in here?"

"Well, yes," Annie replied, puzzled by his question. "Why do you ask?"

He shrugged and hitched his backpack higher on his shoulder. "No reason. It's just that…well, nobody's planted a garden since Mom died."

"Oh," she murmured, understanding now why Jase had seemed so upset when she'd asked his permission to plant a garden. "I didn't know."

Clay shrugged again. "No big deal. It's just dirt."

Annie stared at the weed-clogged clods she'd managed to overturn, suspecting that, though the garden might be nothing more than dirt to Clay, it represented a great deal more to the boy's father.

Feeling the guilt nudging at her for the painful memories her request must have drawn for Jase, she shrugged it off and forced a smile as she turned to Clay. "Are you hungry?"

He reared back and patted his stomach, grinning. "Starving."

Annie caught Rachel's hand, then slung an arm over Clay's shoulders, heading both children toward the house. "How about some rabbit food?" she teased.

"Just call me Thumper," he replied, grinning.

"Clay!"

Clay spun, his grin fading when he saw his father standing in the barn's doorway, scowling, his arms folded across his chest. "Yeah, Dad?" he called.

"You've got chores waiting."

"But couldn't I eat something first?"

When his father merely angled his head and arched a brow in warning, Clay heaved a sigh. "Yes, sir," he mumbled, then turned to Annie. "Sorry. Guess I'll have to grab something later."

Offering him a sympathetic smile, Annie slipped the backpack from his shoulder and lifted it to her own. "I'll save some dip for you," she promised.

As she watched Clay trudge toward the barn, she glanced Jase's way and saw that he waited in the doorway still wearing the now-familiar scowl...and wondered how much of the man's gruffness was direct fallout from the loss of his wife.

"Could I crank up the rototiller and plow up the garden for Annie?"

Hunkered down beside the engine he was working on, Jase glanced up at Clay's question, then frowned and turned his attention back to the spark plug he was adjusting. "You've got chores to do."

"But afterwards?" Clay persisted. "It wouldn't

take me long and it'll take her forever to clean out all those weeds using just a hoe.''

''There's more important work that needs to be done than tilling a garden.''

''Like what?''

At the frustration he heard in his son's voice, Jase dropped the wrench to his knee and glanced up, his frown deepening. ''Like the fence that needs mending down in the bottom. The new calves I hauled in last night that need feeding and watering. The well house that needs painting.''

Ducking his head, Clay scuffed the toe of his boot at the loose hay in the alleyway. ''There's *always* work that needs doing around here,'' he mumbled.

Jase pushed his hands against his knees and rose. ''And there always will be,'' he said, tossing the wrench to the workbench, ''so long as you complain about your chores instead of just doing them.''

''I'm not complaining,'' Clay argued. ''I just wanted to help Annie out.''

''If the new nanny wants a garden, then she'll have to do the work herself.''

''You won't let me help her because you don't like her.''

Jase dug through the tools, reluctant to admit there might be some truth in his son's accusation. ''I didn't say that.''

''You didn't have to. But *we* like her. She's nice. And she's really funny, too. She's always saying stuff or doing stuff that makes us laugh.''

Yeah, Jase thought, keeping his back to his son. He'd noticed those qualities in her, too. As well as a few others. "Whether she's nice or not, isn't the point. Getting your chores done *is*."

Clay's voice took on a pleading tone. "Don't run her off, Dad. Please? We like her."

Jase spun to look at his son. "Run her off? Where'd you get a crazy notion like that?"

Clay lifted a shoulder. "I don't know. But if you're mean to her, she won't want to stay around here long."

Which might be best for them all, Jase affirmed silently, then narrowed a suspicious eye at his son. "You wouldn't have a crush on the new nanny, would you?"

Heat flamed on Clay's cheeks. "Heck no! She's way too old for me."

Jase turned back to the workbench. "You wouldn't be the first male to fall head over bootheels for an older woman. She's young and fairly attractive. "

"*Fairly* attractive?" Clay echoed. "Dad, she's a hottie!"

Jase angled his head to look at his son, his brow furrowing. "Hottie?"

"Well, yeah," Clay said, his cheeks turning a brighter red. "A looker. You know...a babe."

Shocked to discover that his son was aware of the finer points of the opposite sex, Jase picked up a wrench, and began to clean it. "You shouldn't be noticing things like that," he said gruffly.

Chase snorted a laugh. "Shoot. I'd have be to blind *not* to notice."

Irritated by his son's obvious attraction to the nanny, but unsure why, Jase gave his chin a jerk toward the door. "Best get after those chores."

Clay stuffed his hands in his pockets and turned away. ''Yes, sir,'' he mumbled dejectedly.

Jase angled his head to watch his son pull the feed bucket from its nail on the wall and noticed for the first time the slight swell of muscles on the boy's arms, the length of his stride as he headed for the barn door.

Frowning, he stared after him, wondering what had happened to the pint-size kid with the gangly legs and the too-long arms. The one who had always claimed girls were stupid.

The one who had once looked up at his daddy with hero worship in his eyes.

Jase had never considered his house small. Fact was, his home was a spacious two-story built by his parents prior to his own birth, and could adequately accommodate a family of ten or more without putting a hardship on anyone in the house.

But ever since the new nanny's arrival, his house seemed to have shrunk to the size of a cracker box, as had the rest of his ranch. He couldn't take a step without running into her. Literally.

He couldn't count the number of times he'd bumped into her in the house or when stepping out of the barn, which invariably led to physical contact of some description. A hand on her arm to steady her, or one of her hands braced against his chest to prevent him from mowing her down on those occasions when he'd round a corner unaware of her presence.

And those brief, physical contacts were beginning to get on his nerves.

He'd known he wasn't going to like having a

stranger in his house. He'd known, too, that having one who was so young and who was…well…such a *hottie* as his son had described her, might create a problem or two. But he *hadn't* been prepared for the amount of time he would waste thinking about her instead of working, wondering where she was, what she was doing, what she was wearing.

As far as he'd been able to determine, her wardrobe consisted of cutoff jeans, tank tops and other equally revealing articles of clothing. If that wasn't distracting enough, he'd discovered she had a habit of humming while she worked that never failed to draw his gaze…and usually to a part of her anatomy that he had no business looking at.

And tonight was no exception.

With the kids already in bed for the night, he and Annie had the downstairs to themselves. And, though he kept his face hidden behind the newspaper he was reading, he was painfully aware of her exact location, which was, at the moment, less than five feet from his recliner and the tips of his boots. A laundry basket at her side, she sat on the floor folding towels…and humming an irritatingly cheerful little tune.

She glanced up, caught him staring and cocked her head, a questioning smile curving her lips. He quickly ducked his head behind the paper again and flipped the page, pretending to be engrossed in the day's news.

After a moment, he worked up the courage to peek over the top of the newspaper again and caught her just as she rocked up on one hip to stretch to place a folded towel onto the growing stack at her side. At the movement, the hem of her shorts crawled higher on her leg, revealing the thin, white elastic band of her panties and a peek of the lighter-toned skin on her rump that the sun hadn't seen. A low moan rose in his throat, as he stared, all but strangled by the sight.

"Did you say something?"

He snapped his gaze to hers, unaware that he'd let the sound escape. He jerked the paper back in front of his face to hide the heat crawling up his neck. "No," he mumbled. "I...I was just commenting on the weather report for tomorrow. Supposed to be in the high eighties again."

"Eighties," she repeated and sank back on her elbows with a long-suffering sigh. "Hard to believe it's only March. I can't imagine what the temperatures will be by the time summer gets here."

If the temperatures proved to be anything like the heat currently registering in his body, Jase couldn't imagine, either.

Aware of the uncomfortable swell in his jeans, he knew he'd best leave while he was still able to walk.

She glanced up as he rose. "Are you going to bed?" she asked in surprise.

"Yeah," he growled and pivoted quickly, heading for his room.

"Sweet dreams," she called after him.

Yeah, right, he thought irritably. As if his dreams would be anything but X-rated, an affliction he could trace directly back to the day he'd arrived home and found the new nanny in his house.

Annie knew she had a let-me-kiss-it-and-make-it-better tendency that had gotten her into trouble more than once over the years. But knowing that about herself didn't stop her from trying to think of ways to resolve the problems she saw building in the Rawley household.

In the week since Jase's return home, she had watched Tara go from a talkative and spirited young girl to a sullen-faced, headed-for-trouble teenager, who spent more time in her room than she did with her family. While Clay, on the other hand, had metamorphosed from an easygoing, if a bit shy, teenaged boy into a bundle of tightly wound nerves who jumped at the slightest noise, as if he expected a bomb to go off at any minute. And, Rachel, bless her heart, who had tagged Annie's every step since Annie's arrival, soaking up every smile sent her way, every bit of praise, had begun to cling to Annie's legs as if she expected Annie to disappear, leaving her all alone.

Though Annie tried to find another explanation for the sudden changes in the children's behavior, she could find nothing to attribute them to other than their father's return, a realization that both saddened and frustrated her.

Not having a family of her own, Annie knew the value of familial relationships and hated to see Jase and his children not taking advantage of all they had to offer each other. But what could she do to wake them up to what all they were missing?

"You're not God," she reminded herself as she checked her camera for film. "You're just the nanny."

Hoping to find some subjects or scenes to photograph that would take her mind off the Rawleys' problems, she slipped her camera strap over her head and headed outdoors.

Jase stepped inside the barn, paused a moment to let his eyes adjust to the sudden change in light, then headed straight for his workbench. Finding the tool he needed to adjust the carburetor on his truck, he curled his fingers around it, then paused, listening, when he heard a rustling sound above. He glanced up at the rafters that supported the hayloft, then swore, dropping his head and blinking furiously when dust and bits of hay showered down on his face.

Dragging an arm across his eyes, he rammed the wrench into his back pocket and strode for the ladder to the loft, muttering under his breath, "If that damn skunk is back again..."

He climbed the ladder and poked his head through the narrow opening that led to the loft, glancing around. Seeing nothing out of the ordinary, he carefully navigated the last few steps, trying to keep his movements as quiet as possible, so as not to frighten the skunk. It would be just his luck to get sprayed by the varmint, he thought irritably.

Tiptoeing, he made his way along the narrow pathway created by the tall stacks of baled hay he'd stored there the previous summer, peering into the shadowed crevices. When he reached the end without finding a sign of the critter, he started back, but stopped when he heard a soft whirring sound.

Frowning, he turned and retraced his steps, then paused, listening again. Sure that the sound had come from behind the last row of hay, he wedged himself into the space between the hay and the barn wall, and edged his way to the end, silently cursing the loft's oppressive heat that had his shirt sticking to his skin. When he reached the opposite end, he peered out…and nearly choked at the sight that greeted him. Annie lay sprawled on her stomach on the loft floor, her bare feet kicked up in the air, holding a camera before her face.

"What the hell are you doing!"

"Sshh!" she hissed, flapping a warning hand behind her.

Scowling, he stooped to keep from bumping his head on the low rafters and moved to hunker down at her side. He followed the direction of the camera lens to the far corner of the loft where dust motes danced a slow waltz in a slanted beam of sunlight.

"Well, I'll be damned," he murmured as he met the unblinking scrutiny of a mama cat who lay curled on a busted bale of hay.

Easing down to his hips, he drew up his knees, dropped his forearms over them and watched, enchanted by the squirming mass of kittens that suckled greedily at the mama cat's swollen teats. The camera continued to click and whir at his ear, recording the event, frame by frame.

A hand grasped his and he glanced up, surprised to discover that Annie had risen. Smiling, she pressed a finger to her lips to silence him, then tugged him to his feet and led him back through the tunnel of hay.

When she reached the loft's opening, she released his hand to grasp the ladder's braces and grinned up at him as she started down. "Wasn't that just the coolest thing you've ever seen?"

Coolest? Jase shook his head at her choice of adjective as he followed her down. "Yeah, it was cool all right," he muttered wryly, thinking the comment sounded more like something his thirteen-year-old daughter would say than a twenty-six-year-old woman.

"Do you think we should bring them a blanket and some food?" she asked, her eyes all but glowing with excitement, as he dropped down onto the alleyway beside her.

"She's a mouser," he said, scowling. "A barn cat. She knows how to take care of herself."

"But—"

"No," he ordered firmly.

Sighing her disappointment, she lifted the camera over her head, shaking her hair free of the strap. With her arms stretched up high over her head, Jase couldn't help but notice that her T-shirt was damp with perspiration and clung to her skin. Once he noticed that, it was impossible for him not to look closer and see that she wasn't wearing a bra, an absence clearly discernable by the jut of rigid nipples centered over twin mounds of flesh that strained against the T-shirt's damp fabric.

Weakened by the sight, he could only stare, unable to move, unable to think, unable to breathe.

"The light was absolutely perfect," he heard her say as she dropped to a knee to clamp the cover back over her lens. "And those kittens! Weren't they just the most adorable things you've ever seen?"

Jase swallowed hard, weakened further by the glimpse of bare breasts she'd unknowingly revealed when she'd dropped down at his feet to fiddle with her camera. Unable to tear his gaze away from the enticing sight, but knowing that a response of some kind was required, he murmured absently, "Yeah, adorable," then clamped his lips together to stifle the moan that rose as he watched a thin trickle of sweat begin to slowly wind its way down between her breasts.

She glanced up at the mournful sound, caught him staring, then looked down at her front. Obviously aware of what held his attention so raptly, she heaved a sigh and pushed to her feet. "Well, I guess I won't have to worry about you entering me in any wet T-shirt contests."

Distracted by the bob of her breasts as she rose, he shifted his gaze to hers and frowned. "What?"

She chuckled self-consciously and shoved the camera strap over her shoulder. "I said, I guess I won't have to worry about you entering me in any wet T-shirt contests. No big deal," she said with a shrug. "Literally," she added, then laughed.

"Personally, I've always considered anything more than a handful a waste."

Jase wasn't sure what made him state his preference, but when Annie replied with a sassy, "lucky me," he realized that her cheekiness was a front to hide her self-consciousness over her less-than-voluptuous breasts. He stepped closer and slipped his fingers beneath the camera strap, angling it higher on her shoulder. "No," he corrected and arched a brow as he met her gaze. "Lucky *me*."

He watched her green eyes sharpen, then darken, and felt the heat that all but crackled between their bodies. With his fingers still curled around the strap at her shoulder, he slid his gaze to her mouth. Her tongue darted out to slick slowly over her lips and his groin tightened in response.

He wet his own suddenly dry lips and wondered what it would be like to kiss her, what taste and textures he'd find on that impudent mouth of hers. Mortified by the direction of his thoughts, he glanced up…but found the same question burning in her eyes.

He wasn't sure who moved first—him or Annie— but the point became moot when their lips touched. Lightly at first, hesitantly, then slamming together with an urgency that rocked him to the soles of his boots. Was it him, he wondered dazedly, who pushed for more? Or was it Annie?

Didn't matter, he told himself as he closed his hands around her upper arms, intending to push her way, to end this madness before it got out of hand. And he would have ended it, too, if she hadn't chosen that exact moment to wind her arms around his neck and slip her tongue between his lips.

He inhaled sharply as her flavor shot through him, her tongue dancing over his. This is wrong, he told himself even as he gathered her into the circle of his arms. She was young, his children's nanny. He had no business messing around with her in this way.

But no amount of reasoning could bring him to release her, could persuade him to drag his mouth from hers. It had been too long since he'd held a woman, felt feminine softness pressed against the rigid length of his sex. Too long since he'd sipped at a woman's unique sweetness, grown drunk on her flavor alone.

He roamed his hands over her back, down along her curves, stunned by the varying terrains he en-

countered, in the silkiness of her skin, in the heat that
rose from her body to warm his hands. He drank from
her like a man rescued from a desert after being lost
there for weeks. Greedily. Hungrily. Desperate to satisfy a ravenous thirst.

And when a moan of frustration rumbled low in
her throat and she pressed herself more insistently
against him, he thrust his tongue deeply into her
mouth, seeking a release from the need that ripped
through him like a flash of summer lightning.

He wanted her, he realized with a suddenness that
had him gripping her more tightly. All of her. And
nothing short of dragging her to the barn floor and
taking her would satisfy that want.

The realization brought reality crashing down upon
him, making him aware of what he was doing, and
who he was doing it with. He tore his mouth from
hers and stumbled back a step, his chest heaving as
he stared down at her flushed face, her passion-glazed
eyes. Dropping his arms from around her, he whirled
away from the sight of her lips, swollen from the
demanding pressure of his own. He dragged the back
of his hand across his mouth, wanting to rid himself
of her tempting taste. "I'm sorry," he said and curled
his traitorous hands into fists at his sides.

"I'm not."

He spun, startled by her reply. "What?"

She tucked her fingers around the camera strap and
lifted her shoulder in a shrug. "I'm not sorry."

"But...why?"

"You're a good kisser," she said simply, then
smiled and added with a wink, "And I've always ap-

preciated a man who really knows how to cut loose and kiss a woman.''

As he stared, dumbstruck, she headed for the barn door. ''By the way,'' she called, turning and walking backwards. ''If you ever want to cut loose again, just give me a holler. I'll be around.'' Waggling her fingers at him, she turned and strode from the barn, humming that same disgustingly cheerful tune.

Three

Jase had never had trouble sleeping...or at least he hadn't since he'd figured out that physical exhaustion was an excellent cure for the particular form of insomnia he had suffered since his wife's death. But on this particular night, and in spite of the fourteen hours of backbreaking labor he'd put in on his ranch, his cure didn't seem to be working. He hadn't even taken a break for dinner, convinced there was no way in hell he could face his housekeeper across the dinner table. Not after what had transpired between them that afternoon. Not after he'd kissed her. Not after he'd felt that hard, firm body of hers pressed against his.

Not after her assurance that she'd be around if he ever felt the need to kiss a woman again.

Swearing, he rolled from his bed and paced across the room, dragging a hand over his hair. He had to quit thinking about her. Had to shake the images that kept leaping to mind. The feel of her in his arms. Plump, moist lips that surrendered beneath his, even as they demanded a satisfaction of their own. The little muffled whimpers of pleasure that hummed low in her throat. The small, firm breasts flattened against his chest, the prod of desire-thickened nipples. The feel of her buttock muscles tightening in his—

He spun, swearing again. He had to quit thinking like this! About *her!* She was trouble with a capital T. He'd known that from the first moment he'd laid eyes on her. For two long years he'd managed to suppress his need for physical release with a woman, but after little more than a week with the new nanny in his house, all he could think about was getting her into bed.

Grabbing his jeans, he jerked them on. There was only one way to handle this, he told himself as he headed for the bedroom door, yanking up his zipper. He had to fire her. Get her out of his house. If he didn't, he was going to go stark raving mad...or have her. And he refused to fall prey to either of those possibilities.

A man on a mission, he marched down the hall, through the darkened kitchen and bounded up the staircase. At the landing, he made a sharp turn to the right and rapped his knuckles against her bedroom door.

He heard a rustling sound from the other side and a mumbled "Just a minute." Scowling, he folded his arms across his chest and waited.

Seconds later, the door opened and Annie appeared, shrugging on a robe.

Framed by the golden light of the bedside lamp she'd switched on, she squinted sleepily up at him. "Is something wrong?" she asked as she tugged the belt of her robe around her waist.

"Yeah," he said, infuriated to discover that she could sleep, when he could do nothing but toss and turn and think about her. "We need to have a talk."

She swept a hand over her hair, holding it back from her face as she peered up at him curiously. "What about?"

He glanced down the hallway and to the rooms where his children slept, then returned his gaze to hers. "Can we talk inside? I don't want to wake the kids."

"Well, yes," she said clearly puzzled by the odd request, but stepped aside, allowing him to enter.

After casting another nervous glance down the hallway, he closed the door behind him. He paused, watching as she crossed to the bed and sat down. He bit back a frustrated groan as all the images he'd tried to block returned, flashing across his mind like freeze frames from an erotic movie. She shouldn't look this good, he told himself. It just wasn't normal. Hell! He'd awakened her in the middle of the night from a dead sleep, yet she looked good enough to eat, sitting there in a ratty terry bathrobe with those toenails of hers, still painted a putrid blue, peeking from beneath its hem. "You're going to have to leave," he blurted out.

Her eyes widened in surprise. "What?"

He waved a frustrated hand. "You're going to have to leave. This just isn't working out."

She rose slowly, her cheeks flushing with anger,

her green eyes snapping with it. "For who? You? Or the children?"

"For anybody!" he cried, his voice rising in frustration. "I'll give you a month's severance pay and a good reference, if you need one, but I want you out of here first thing in the morning."

She drew the folds of her robe's collar together high on her neck, and lifted her chin. "I don't want any more from you than what is owed me, and you can keep your reference, good or bad."

Seeing the tears gleaming in her eyes and knowing he was responsible for them, Jase dragged a hand over his head, mussing his wild hair even more. "Look," he said, feeling like a heel. "Don't take this personally."

Her nostrils flared. "If my termination isn't personal, then I'd like to know what it is. I've done my job. You certainly can't find fault with me there. I've cared for the children and supervised their activities, just as your sister instructed. I've cooked for them, done their laundry, settled their disputes and managed to keep the house clean and neat, as well."

Though he tried, Jase couldn't find an argument in there anywhere. "You're young," he said, digging for a reasonable excuse she might accept, and bit back a groan when her chin shot higher. "Well, hell, you *are* young!" he shouted.

"There isn't that much difference in your sister's and my ages, and you didn't seem to have a problem leaving your children in her care."

"That's because she's my sister, dammit, and I was never tempted to throw my sister down on the barn floor and have my way with her!"

"Dad?"

Jase whirled to find Clay standing in the doorway, a pair of cotton pajama bottoms riding low on his hips, his hair spiked from sleep. With his eyes narrowed suspiciously, the boy leaned to peer around his father at Annie.

Jase immediately took a step sideways to block his son's view, wondering how much of their conversation Clay had overheard. "What are you doing out of bed?" he snapped. "You should be asleep."

Clay jerked his gaze to his father's, his expression turning accusing. "Why are you in Annie's room?"

"We're talking."

"You were yelling at her," Clay argued. "I heard you."

Annie stepped from behind Jase, touched by the boy's concern. "I'm fine, Clay," she reassured him. "Go on back to bed. I can handle this."

The teenager shifted his gaze from Annie to his father, then back, his reluctance to leave obvious. "Tara's sick," he mumbled.

Annie's eyes shot wide. "What?" she cried, hurrying forward. "What's wrong with her?"

Clay rolled a shoulder and turned away. "I don't know. I heard her in the bathroom puking, but she's got the door locked and won't let me in."

Annie and Jase bolted for the door, shoving impatiently at each other as they both tried to wedge their way through the opening at the same time. Frustrated, Annie managed to twist her way past him and ran down the hall. At the bathroom door, she stopped and pressed her ear against the wood, listening.

"Tara?" she called softly. "Sweetheart, it's Annie. Are you ill?"

Jase shouldered her aside and lifted a hand to pound his fist against the door. "Open up, Tara!" he shouted. "Now!"

Annie pressed her lips together and shot him a disapproving look. "You're only going to upset her with your shouting," she whispered angrily.

"That's too damn bad." He closed a hand over the doorknob and gave it a hard twist. "You have exactly three seconds to open this door, Tara," he yelled, "or I'm getting my tools and taking it off its hinges. One. Two. Thr—"

The door flew open and Tara stepped out, her arms folded over her chest in a belligerent stance Annie had grown accustomed to since Jase's return.

"Are you sick?" Jase demanded to know.

"What do you care?" she muttered and turned for her room.

Jase caught her by the arm and spun her back around. "Clay said you were sick. Are you?"

Tara shot her brother a murderous look. "Tattletale."

Jase gave her arm a shake. "Are you sick or not?"

Slowly, Tara turned her gaze to her father, her eyes flat with resentment. "No."

"But I heard you puking," Clay argued.

Tara shot him another dark look. "So I threw up. Big deal. Something I ate probably didn't agree with me, because I feel fine now."

Annie listened to the exchange, an ugly suspicion rising in her mind when she saw a toothbrush lying on the floor near the base of the toilet.

Jase, on the other hand, seemed relieved by his daughter's reassurance that she wasn't ill. "Good," he said and released her arm. "Y'all get back to bed and go to sleep."

He waited until the twins had returned to their rooms and closed their doors, then turned to Annie, his scowl returning. "We'll finish our discussion downstairs."

Annie darted a worried glance at Tara's door. "I'll be down in a minute. I just want to check on Tara first and make sure she's all right."

"Make it snappy," Jase muttered and headed for the stairs.

Annie slipped into the bathroom, retrieved the toothbrush, then crossed to Tara's door. She tapped softly, then waited, praying she was wrong.

Tara opened the door, still wearing the same belligerent expression. "What do you want?"

Annie opened her hand, revealing the toothbrush. "I found this on the floor in the bathroom."

A look of alarm flashed across Tara's eyes before she hid it behind a mask of indifference. "I probably knocked it off the basin when I was sick." She snatched the toothbrush from Annie's hand and, with a muttered thanks, slammed the door in her face.

Annie stared at the door for a moment, then turned and marched downstairs and to the kitchen where Jase waited, slouched in his chair at the head of the table. She crossed to her own chair opposite his and sank down. Unable to keep her suspicions to herself a moment longer, she said, "She's lying."

He peered at her in confusion. "Who's lying?"

"Tara." Annie sank back against her chair and

pressed a hand against her stomach, feeling a little bit sick herself at the thought of the harm the girl could be doing to her body if Annie's suspicions were correct.

"Why would she lie about throwing up? She said she ate something that didn't agree with her, threw it up and now she's fine. Sounds reasonable enough to me."

Annie inhaled deeply, searching for the right words, knowing how important it was for her to make Jase understand the seriousness of the situation. "Yes, she threw up," she agreed. "And, yes, she feels fine now. But she didn't throw up because of something she ate. She *made* herself throw up."

"And why the hell would she do a stupid thing like that?"

"To get your attention."

He slumped down in his chair, scowling. "That's the wildest bunch of bull I've ever heard. Who in their right mind would make themselves throw up just to get some attention?"

Annie leaned forward, determined to make him understand Tara's need for him. "A teenage girl who is desperate to make her father notice her, that's who. She's thirteen, Jase. The time in a young girl's life when her hormones are in a constant state of flux. The time when her emotions can run the gamut from ecstatic joy to darkest depression in the blink of an eye. The time," she added pointedly, "when a young girl needs the love and support of her parents the very most."

Jase rocketed from his chair and turned away, pacing from the table. "She's only got one parent," he growled. "Me. And she knows I love her."

"How does she know?" Annie challenged. "Do you tell her?

He yanked open the refrigerator, scowling. "She knows," he muttered as he fished through the refrigerator's contents for a soft drink.

"But do you *tell* her?" Annie insisted.

He slammed the refrigerator door and ripped back the tab on the canned drink. He tipped his head back, guzzling the soda, then dropped his hand to aim the can at Annie's nose. "I don't need you, or anybody else, telling me how to raise my own kids."

"That's not my intent," she replied as she rose. "But are you familiar with bulimia?"

"Tara isn't bulimic. Hell," he said, gesturing wildly with the can, "she's skinny as a rail, as it is. There'd be no reason for her to make herself sick just to lose weight."

"I didn't say she *was* bulimic. But last week she mentioned to me that they were studying eating disorders in her health class and discussed the warning signs for both anorexia and bulimia. She seemed intrigued by the possibility that a person could suffer from bulimia and no one who lived with them would even be aware of the problem."

Annie glanced down at her hands, twisting her fingers nervously, knowing she was overstepping her bounds, but helpless to do anything else. "I think she's testing you," she said quietly, then found the courage to look back up at him. "She's trying to prove to herself that you really don't care anything for her."

"That's ridiculous. I care for my daughter."

"Whether you do or not really isn't the point. It's how Tara *perceives* your feelings that's important. And from what I've observed, she considers your indifference and the time you spend away from the house as a lack of affection for her."

"So what do you suggest I do? Ignore the work that needs to be done on the ranch? Stay in the house all day and play dolls with her?"

"Tara doesn't play with dolls any longer. But, no, that's not what I'm suggesting. I'm simply trying to point out that Tara is a troubled teen who needs her father's love and support more than she ever has before. What concerns me most is the lengths she might go to gain your attention."

He gave his chair an angry shove, slamming it back up to the table. "Well, thankfully, you're leaving and won't have to concern yourself with Tara's welfare any longer."

"Do you really think replacing me at this point in time is wise?"

He braced his hands on his hips and narrowed his eyes at her. "So that's it. It's your own welfare you're concerned about, not Tara's."

Annie fought back the anger that rose, the urge to strike back, and forced herself to focus instead on Tara's needs. "She lost her mother," she reminded him. "And now her aunt is gone, too, the only other woman in her life she felt close to. I don't think it would be in Tara's best interest for me to leave right now. She's accepted me, as have the other children, and I'm afraid another change in the household so soon after Penny leaving would be upsetting for them all. Especially Tara. She might decide to run away or...worse.''

He stared at her, the blood slowly draining from his face, obviously understanding the danger Annie hadn't been able to bring herself to voice. Swallowing hard, he turned away and crossed to the sink, bracing his hands on its edge as he stared blindly at the dark window. ''You really think the situation is that bad?''

''I don't know,'' Annie admitted honestly. ''But she's definitely going through a rebellious stage, and the statistics for troubled teens who attempt suicide are alarming. What she needs right now is stability, close supervision...and love.''

He dropped his chin to his chest, groaning, and the sound tore through Annie's heart. In spite of his obvious dislike for her, his intent to remove her from his home, she found herself wanting to cross to him, wrap her arms around him and offer him her comfort. Before she could give in to the temptation, though, he lifted his head, his expression bleak as he stared at the dark window.

''Stay, then,'' he said in a voice rough with emotion. ''I can't take a chance on losing my daughter, too.''

Annie had the opportunity to question the wisdom of her insistence to be allowed to remain in the Rawley household more than once over the next few days. Ever since the late-night confrontation between Tara and her father, Tara seemed to have withdrawn even more from the family unit, a situation that concerned Annie more and more each day.

And Jase. The man had to be the blindest, most

stubborn man in the world. In spite of Annie's warnings, he continued to spend the majority of his time out on the ranch, doing whatever he did while away from the house and all but ignoring his children, as well as Annie.

But she couldn't give up, she told herself as she headed outdoors to the garden, intending to take out her frustrations on the weeds that grew there. It didn't matter to Annie that Jase avoided *her*. She was a mature woman and could handle rejection, though she did find his determination to deny his obvious attraction to her puzzling—and a bit frustrating, since she found him so attractive. But what mattered a great deal to her was his avoidance of his family. She *had* to find a way to draw them back together, she told herself. For their sakes. How she'd go about doing that, she wasn't sure. But she was confident she'd find a way.

As she neared the garden, she slowed, then stopped altogether, her mouth sagging open when she saw that the weed-choked ground had been plowed under and turned into neatly aligned rows. She glanced at the rototiller parked near the fence…and knew who had done the work.

Jase. He'd plowed the garden for her. But why?

The sound of cattle bawling drew her gaze to the corral where Jase had worked all morning. Dust hung like a cloud over the area, stirred by the calves' constant milling inside. She caught a glimpse of Jase moving among the animals, his hat grayed by a thin film of dust, his shirt clinging wetly to his back and chest beneath the relentless afternoon sun. The calves moved in a tight herd away from him, obviously distrusting the human in their midst.

She strained for a better look, wondering what he was doing, and wondering, too, if she dared interrupt his work long enough to thank him for plowing the garden for her. While she wavered uncertainly, a dog barked and she shifted her gaze to the Australian shepherd dog, sitting at the gate. The animal's posture was tense and expectant, as if anxious to join Jase inside the corral.

As Annie stared, mesmerized by the scene, she realized what a wonderful photo op this would be and raced for the house. She returned minutes later, fitting a zoom lens over her camera. As she neared the corral, she slowed her steps, not wanting to disrupt the action going on inside. Drawing a deep breath to steady her hands, she stooped and placed the camera's lens between the pipes that shaped the corral. She quickly brought the dog into focus and managed to squeeze off several shots before the milling calves blocked her view.

Pleased, she readjusted the angle of the camera and focused in on Jase. The zoom lens brought him within touching distance, giving her an intimate view of the dark stains of sweat on his shirt, the dust that filled the creases on his face, the determined set of his jaw. Rugged, she thought, pressing her finger excitedly over the shutter release time and time again. Man pitted against animal. Contemporary cowboy. Hardworking rancher.

If the pictures turned out nearly as well as she hoped, she would send them to an editor of one of the Western or livestock magazines for consideration.

With the focus for the series and potential markets tumbling through her mind, she kept the camera focused on Jase, recording his movements, the range of emotions that swept across his face. Steely-eyed determination, she thought with a shiver. A sharp wariness in the squint of his eyes when a calf squared off with him, threatening head-to-head battle. Smug pleasure when he managed to separate from the herd the steer he wanted. She clicked off several more shots, only vaguely aware of the flutter of attraction that warmed her belly.

"Roscoe!"

The dog bounded forward at Jase's sharp command, his tongue lolling, his tail wagging.

Jase waved a hand in what Annie assumed was a signal of some sort and the dog dropped to the ground and slunk surreptitiously in a wide circle around the steer, approaching the animal from the rear. With a slow, methodic diligence, the dog pushed the steer toward an open chute. When the steer darted inside, Jase moved quickly to drop the gate into place, successfully penning the animal.

Annie squeezed off a couple of more shots, then straightened. "Wow," she said breathlessly, impressed.

Jase whipped his head around at the sound of her voice, obviously unaware of her presence until that moment. Frowning, he dropped his gaze to the camera she held at her waist. "What the hell are you doing with that?" he asked impatiently.

She smiled, determined not to let his grouchiness chase her away. "Taking some pictures. Great action. Lots of emotion, too."

His frown deepened into a scowl. "It's called work," he muttered and stretched to draw a large stainless-steel syringe from a toolbox on the ground near the chute.

Annie hurried over to peer through the rails. "What are you doing?" she asked, already drawing the camera before her face.

"Vaccinating the calves." Jase rubbed his fingers high on the calf's shoulder, pinched an area of flesh between his fingers, then injected the needle.

Annie clicked a shot, then winced when the calf bawled. "Did you hurt him?" she asked, lowering the camera.

"No. He's just pissed because I separated him from his buddies."

"Oh," she said doubtfully, not at all convinced the calf hadn't experienced a little pain. When Jase picked up a tool that looked something like pliers, she pushed to the balls of her feet, straining for a better view. "What's that for?"

"I use it to notch his ear."

Annie hunched her shoulders, tensing, as Jase positioned the tool over the calf's ear and squeezed. "Surely *that* hurts him," she said, grimacing as Jase removed a small V of flesh.

He tossed a look of disgust over his shoulder, then rammed the tool into his back pocket without bothering to comment.

"Why do you notch his ear?" she persisted, figuring she'd need some factual data for the article she planned to write to accompany the photos.

"It's a way to identify him."

"I thought ranchers branded their cattle?"

He inhaled deeply, obviously annoyed by her questions. "I do, but only those animals I plan to add to my herd. These are stocker calves. I'll feed 'em out, then sell most of 'em before winter comes. Those I keep, I'll brand."

"Oh," she said, absorbing that information. "But—"

Before she could ask the next question, he turned to scowl at her. "Don't you have anything better to do than stand around all day, asking a bunch of stupid questions?"

Annie thought of the work she'd planned to do in the garden and that which awaited her in the house, and slipped her hand behind her back, crossing two fingers. "No. Not a thing," she lied cheerfully.

He jerked his chin toward the truck parked beside the corral. "Then make yourself useful and fetch that clipboard from the front seat."

Excited at the thought of assisting, she tugged her camera from around her neck and jogged for the truck. Placing the camera carefully on the seat, she grabbed the requested clipboard and hurried back to the chute. "Here you go," she said, sticking an arm between the pipes to pass Jase the clipboard.

With his hands occupied with the calf, he gave his head a jerk, motioning her inside. "Bring it over here."

With a nervous glance at the other calves that continued to mill in a tight group in the corral, Annie swung a leg through the rails, then ducked her head and slipped through the space, straightening to stand on the other side. Keeping a cautious eye on the calves, she sidestepped her way to where Jase waited.

"Here," she said and thrust the clipboard in what she hoped was his direction.

"Tag number 12, Black Angus, steer."

Annie whipped her head around to peer at him in confusion. "What?"

"Tag number 12, Black Angus, steer," he repeated impatiently, then ordered, "Write it down."

"Oh," she said and drew the clipboard to her hip, balancing it there as she drew the pen from its holder. She quickly jotted down the information, casting an occasional nervous glance toward the other calves.

"Got it?"

"Yes," she said and exhaled an uneasy breath.

He released his hold on the steer and dragged his hands across the seat of his pants. "Put today's date in the column marked Vaccinated."

She quickly made the entry, then hugged the clipboard to her breasts. "Is that all?"

He gave his chin a jerk in response as he released the gate. "For that one."

Annie's eyes widened as she turned to stare at the herd. There had to be at least thirty or forty calves remaining. "You mean we have to do *all* of them?"

"All," he confirmed, then pulled up the gate on the chute. "Do you think you could stand in this opening and keep that steer from getting out?"

"Well…yes," she said, eyeing the animal warily. "I suppose so."

"When I give the signal, move out of the way and Roscoe will herd the next calf inside."

Swallowing hard, Annie positioned herself in front of the chute, casting an uneasy glance over her shoulder at the steer who stood at the far end. Suppressing a shudder at his intimidating size, she turned back around to see Jase approaching the herd. She quickly forgot about the steer behind her and watched in growing fascination as Jase moved among the animals, studying them, seemingly unafraid of getting stomped on or gored by an occasional budding horn.

"Get ready," he called, obviously having selected the calf he wanted from the herd. "Roscoe!"

Annie watched the dog shoot forward, then screamed when something struck her hard in the middle of her back, knocking her off her feet. She flung out her arms to break her fall, but slammed face first against the ground, her teeth jarring at the impact. The steer leaped over her, grazing her back with one of his sharp hooves.

"Why the hell did you let him get past you?"

Dazed, she slowly lifted her face from the dirt, blinking twice before she realized what Jase had said. "I didn't *let* him get past me," she cried indignantly, then grimaced and spit a collection of foul-tasting dirt from her mouth.

"You were supposed to block the opening!"

She heaved herself up on her elbows as Jase bore down her, his hands fisted at his sides, his eyes dark with anger. "I *was* blocking the opening," she snapped. "He knocked me down and ran right over the top of me."

"Well, you shouldn't have let him get past you."

She pushed herself to her knees, spitting granules of dirt that clung stubbornly to her lips, and glared up at him. "Look, buster," she said, drawing her hands to her hips. "I'm not Calamity Jane. I stood in the opening, just like you instructed. It isn't *my* fault the dang calf got out.''

"Then whose fault is it?" he shouted, gesturing wildly at the chute behind her. "*You* were the one who was supposed to guard the gate.''

Feeling the anger building, Annie pushed herself the rest of the way to her feet, then gasped, doubling over, as a pain shot across the middle of her back.

"What's the matter?"

She gulped, then swallowed, fighting back the nausea that rose. "I think he stepped on me.''

With her head bent toward the ground, her view of the world was narrowed to the area around her feet. She saw Jase's boots enter that space, then felt the weight of his hand on her hip.

"Where?"

She drew in a shaky breath. "Just above my waist.''

She felt his fingers catch the hem of her tank top, then the brush of his knuckles as he drew it up and away from her spine. When he didn't offer a comment, she squeezed her eyes shut, fearing the worst. "Is it bad?"

When he still didn't reply, she angled her head back over her shoulder to peer at him. The almost apoplectic look on his face took her by surprise.

"Jase?"

He snapped his gaze to hers, heat staining his cheeks. "Uh…no," he replied and dropped his hand from her shirt. "It's just a scrape.''

She pressed her hands against her waist and straightened slowly, groaning. "Tell that to my aching back.''

"I've got a first aid kit in my truck. I'll get it."

She nodded and walked to the side of the corral. Sinking gingerly to the ground, she waited while he went to collect the kit.

When he returned, she lifted her face, squinting up at him as he opened the box. "This isn't going to hurt, is it?"

He hunkered down beside her, balancing the box on his knee as he dug through its contents. "Might sting a little."

She drew back, watching as he set the box aside and tore open a small packet he'd removed. "What's that?" she asked suspiciously.

"A piece of gauze soaked with hydrogen peroxide. I'll need to clean the wound first."

"Wound?" she repeated, snapping up her head to look at him. "I thought you said it was just a scrape."

He tugged his hat down lower over his brow, hiding his eyes from her. "Wound. Scrape. Same damn thing."

"I bet you wouldn't think so if it was *your* back that was hurt," she replied petulantly.

He drew a circle in the air with his finger, indicating for her to turn around.

Frowning, Annie scooted on her bottom, offering him her back. "Just be gentle, okay?" she requested uneasily.

She felt the pressure of his fingers as he lifted her shirt, then cool air hitting her skin as he shoved it up high on her back and held it between her shoulder blades. A second or two passed without any other movement, and she angled her head slightly over her shoulder. "Well? Are you going to clean it, or not?"

"Yeah," he said, his voice suddenly sounding rusty. "I am." He dropped down to his knees and eased closer, his thighs bumping against her hips.

Squeezing her eyes shut, Annie bowed her back to give him easier access and dipped her chin, prepared to scream if he treated her roughly. But the fingers that swept the gauze across her back were surprisingly gentle, almost tender in their ministrations. She flinched a little as the cold liquid struck her warm skin, and he jerked his hand back.

"Did I hurt you?"

She bit back a smile at the alarm she heard in his voice. "No. It's just cold."

"Oh," he said, releasing a breath. He blotted at the scrape, then tossed the square of gauze aside. "I'm going to put some antibiotic cream on it now."

"Whatever you say, Doc."

She heard him digging through the box, then felt the pressure of his fingers again as he gently smoothed the cream over the scrape. The sensation wasn't all that unpleasant, though she did feel a slight sting when the ointment came in contact with her broken skin. She closed her eyes as he continued to stroke, lulled by the slow, almost hypnotic movement of his fingers.

"You might be a little sore tomorrow," he offered quietly.

"Tomorrow?" she echoed, then snorted a laugh. "How about right now?"

"Where does it hurt?"

She stretched an arm around behind her, pointing at a spot just above her waist and below the scrape. "There."

He pressed the tips of his fingers tentatively against the spot.

"Yeah," she said, and closed her eyes again with a sigh. "Right there."

He increased the pressure of his fingertips, gently kneading at the sore muscle. She arched her back, moaning softly, and leaned forward, hugging her arms around her knees to give him better access. She hummed her pleasure as he increased the pressure of his thumbs on either side of her spine, all but purred at the slow stretch of his fingers across the width of her back and shivered deliciously when his fingers dipped into the curve of her waist and gently squeezed.

She was sure he'd stop the massage then, prayed he wouldn't, and caught her lip between her teeth when he shaped his hands around her waist and began to slowly drag his palms up her sides. There was a dreamlike quality to his movements, a studied slowness that made her wonder if he realized what he was doing or who he was doing it to.

He didn't like her. He'd made no bones about that. And she seriously doubted that he was giving her the massage because of any latent sense of responsibility he felt for her soreness. And he certainly wasn't doing it out of the kindness of his heart! As far as she could tell, he didn't have one.

But as his hands continued to stroke upwards, she decided the why wasn't important. The only thing that mattered was the play of his palms over her skin. She emptied her mind of everything, focusing on the strength in the wide hands that shaped her, the gentleness in them, the sensual chafe of his work-roughened palms over her tender flesh. Heat swirled to life low in her belly, swept out to gently nudge nerve endings from sleep.

She shivered when his palms bumped slowly over the rounded sides of her breasts, then sucked in a breath, her eyes flipping wide, when he slipped his hands around her and covered them.

Tensed, she waited, uncertain what to say, what to do. She could hear the rasp of his labored breathing behind her, feel the tremble in the fingers cupping her, recognized both as his struggle for control. Slowly he increased the pressure of his hands, molding them around her breasts' shape, his fingers sinking deeply into their cushiony softness. She closed her eyes as wave after wave of sensation spilled through her and her nerves skipped into a faster dance beneath her skin. A low moan of pleasure crawled up her throat and slipped past her lips before she could stop it.

At the sound, he snatched his hands from around her and bolted to his feet. Startled—and a little disappointed—she twisted her head around to peer up at him, but the glare of the sun prevented her from seeing his face.

"I finished doctoring your scrape," he mumbled as he stooped to scoop the first aid kit from the ground.

That he would try to pretend the intimacy had never occurred, surprised Annie...and infuriated her. She grabbed hold of a rail, hauled herself to her feet and whirled to face him. "Excuse me? Are you just going to pretend that that never happened?"

He glanced her way, and she stumbled back a step,

stunned by the raw need she saw in his eyes, the rigid set of his jaw.

He quickly turned away. "Go back to the house," he growled. "I'll finish the rest of the calves alone."

Four

Jase made it inside the barn and out of sight of the house—and he hoped, Annie—then stopped and, with a furious growl, hurled the first aid kit against the tack-room door. It bounced off the wood with a loud *crack* and its lid popped open, spilling the box's contents out over the alleyway. He stared at the scattered supplies, his chest heaving as if he'd just run a marathon, his body trembling as if he'd just encountered a ghost.

He'd touched her, he thought, his mind spinning crazily at the memory, his pulse still beating erratically from the contact. Dear God, he'd touched Annie.

He opened his hands to stare at them, still able to feel the silk-like texture of her skin, the heat in it as he'd swept his palms up her sides. The pillowed softness of her breasts giving beneath his hands, the jab of desire-awakened nipples growing rigid against his palms.

Groaning, he curled his fingers inward, digging his fingertips painfully into his palms, trying to block the memory, the shame.

No, he thought in self-reproach. He hadn't *touched* her. He'd *groped* her like some hormone-crazed teenager would a date in the back seat of his father's car.

And what angered him even more was that he wished he could touch her again.

He swore and spun, driving his fingers through his hair. He was crazy. He had to be. There was no other way to explain his actions. He knew better. He'd known he was attracted to her. Hadn't he promised himself that he would stay away from her for that very reason? He didn't want to feel anything for her. Hell, he didn't want to feel anything, at all! Feeling *hurt*, and he'd had a stomach full of hurting.

"Jase?"

At the sound of her voice behind him, he groaned, knotting his fingers in his hair. "What do you want?"

"I forgot to thank you for tilling the garden for me."

He inhaled deeply, then dropped his hands and lifted his head to stare at the far wall. "You've said it. So go."

"Why are you so angry with me?"

"I'm not angry."

He heard her short snort of disagreement and wished fervently that she would accept his answer and just leave him the hell alone.

But he knew she wouldn't. Not Annie.

And she didn't.

"Liar."

He dragged in another long breath, trying to force the tension from his body, the sharpness from his tone, hoping if he succeeded in doing so he could convince her to leave. "I said I'm not angry."

"Then why won't you look at me?"

He turned slowly, curling his hands into fists at his sides as he braced himself for the confrontation. "Okay," he said, enunciating each word carefully and distinctly as he met her gaze. "I'm looking at you, and I'm not angry. *Now* are you satisfied?"

She cocked her head to the side. "No," she said, after moment of quiet deliberation. "I'm not." She folded her arms across her chest and walked around him. "Your hands are fisted, a sure sign of agitation. And there's a little muscle ticking right here—" when she reached to point at the spot, he jerked away, dodging her touch "—on your temple," she finished and infuriated him more by biting back a smile.

"Why don't you just go back to the house like I told you to and leave me the hell alone?"

"Because that's not healthy."

He threw his hands up in the air. "For who?" he shouted.

"For you."

He took a threatening step toward her. "Listen, little *girl,*" he said, leveling a finger at her nose. "If you know what's good for you, you'll sashay that cute little fanny of yours back to the house and keep it there."

Her smile widening, she strained to peer over her

shoulder at her backside. "You really think my fanny's cute?"

Jase dropped his face against his hands, moaning.

"Come on, Jase," she cajoled and cupped a hand over the back of his neck, squeezing softly. "Would it really be so bad to admit that you're attracted to me?"

He tried to ignore the gentle urging of her fingers against his neck…but failed, the same as he'd failed in trying to avoid her.

"Would it help if I told you that I'm attracted to you, too?" she asked softly.

Her face was dipped close to his, so close the moist warmth of her breath fanned the shell of his ear and sent a shiver chasing down his spine. He drew in a deep breath, searching for the strength to resist her, and her scent filled his head, making his mind spin dizzily. But it was her quiet admission that put the tremble in his hands, the throbbing ache in his loins.

She was attracted to him. Oh, damn. How was he supposed to respond to that? How was he supposed to resist her, when all he wanted to do was throw her down on the floor and make love to her? Was this some kind of game she was playing with him? Was she purposely trying to seduce him?

Knowing he had to send her away before he completely lost control, he forced his hands from his face and straightened. He met her gaze, sure that he'd find teasing in her eyes, the coy playfulness of a woman with seduction on her mind. But all he found in the green depths was clear-eyed honesty and warm compassion.

He could have resisted coyness, had before when

other women had plied him with their womanly wiles, but her honesty and compassion rendered him helpless. "Annie—" When her hand slipped from behind his neck to rest against his cheek and she tipped her head to the side, her expression softening in understanding, he shut his eyes on a groan and closed his hand over hers. "Don't," he said and dragged her fingers away.

"Jase—"

"Don't," he said more insistently and turned his back on her.

He heard her sigh of defeat but refused to turn around.

"Okay," she said softly. "But someday you're going to have to let go of all that emotion that's inside you. If you don't, you're going to wind up with an ulcer, for sure."

That afternoon Annie waited for the arrival of the school bus, smug in her new discovery.

In spite of Jase's insistence that the mama cat she'd photographed was self-reliant and could take care of herself and her babies, Annie had taken an old blanket and some food to the loft, only to find the cat and her kittens already snuggled on a horse blanket spread over loose hay and containers of water and food nearby.

Knowing it was Jase who had provided for the cat and her babies, she considered confronting him with her knowledge of his kindness...but quickly decided against it. She knew he'd probably just deny the act or attempt to lessen its significance in some way.

The big softy, she thought with a smile as she

watched the bus screech to a stop with a squeal of brakes. Jase wanted her to believe he was mean and callous, but she was beginning to believe that there was another side to him. One that could possibly grow with the proper nurturing.

Pleasure spread warmly through her chest as she watched Jase's children troop toward her, Rachel lagging behind the twins as she stopped to pick wildflowers growing alongside the drive. Heavens, but she loved these kids, she thought as she hurried to meet them.

"How was school?" she asked as she accepted the backpack Clay passed to her.

"Lame," Tara muttered and passed her by.

"Same old same old," Clay replied and turned wearily for the barn.

"Wait," Annie called to Clay. She held out a paper bag. "A snack," she whispered and shot him a conspiratorial wink.

"Peanut butter cookies?" he asked hopefully, sneaking a peek inside.

"They are your favorite, aren't they?"

He glanced up at her, a grin spreading from ear to ear. "Thanks, Annie," he said, then turned and ran for the barn.

Annie smiled after him, but glanced down when she felt a tug on her shirttail.

"Do I get peanut butter cookies, too?" Rachel asked, peering up at her.

"Nope." She laughed at the child's crestfallen expression and dropped to a knee in front of her. Smiling, she tapped a finger against the end of the little girl's nose. "You get oatmeal, because they're *your* favorite."

"What kind does Tara get?"

Annie rose, her gaze going to the house, watching as Tara stepped inside. "Sugar cookies," she replied, secretly hoping the sweet treat would take some of the sourness out of Tara's disposition.

"Daddy doesn't like us."

Annie glanced up from the sandwiches she was making to look at Rachel in surprise. "Well, of course your father likes you."

Rachel stubbornly shook her head, her pigtails slapping against rosy cheeks. "No, he doesn't. Tara said so."

Annie turned to look at Tara who was standing at her opposite side, wrapping in plastic wrap the sandwiches Annie had made. "Did you tell Rachel that, Tara?"

Tara kept her gaze on her work but lifted a shoulder. "So what if I did?" she replied sullenly. "It's the truth."

Annie laid down her knife and turned, catching Tara's shoulders in her hands and angling the girl around to face her. "But your father loves you," she insisted. When Tara refused to look at her, Annie pressed a finger beneath the girl's chin and forced her face up. "He loves you," she said more firmly. "I know he does."

"Then why doesn't he ever spend time with us?"

Her heart breaking at the tears she saw glistening in the girl's eyes, Annie gathered Tara into her arms. "Because he has so much work to do," Annie replied, hugging her. "It takes a lot to run a ranch of this size." Realizing how weak the excuse sounded, especially to a young girl, she pushed Tara out to arm's length and forced a smile. "But maybe we can change that."

"Yeah, right," Tara muttered, and dashed a finger beneath her nose. "Like Dad would quit working, just because we wanted him to."

"He might," Annie said secretively. "Especially if we lure him with a really tasty picnic lunch."

"A picnic?" Rachel cried and began jumping up and down and clapping her hands. "Can we really go on a picnic?"

"Why not?" Annie asked. "Instead of waiting for Clay to come and pick up the sandwiches, we'll just deliver their lunch to the hayfield." She waved a hand toward the pantry. "Tara, you get the picnic basket and, Rachel, you get that tin of cookies we baked this morning."

Within minutes the three had packed the picnic basket and tossed a quilt into the trunk of Annie's car and were headed for the hayfield where Jase and Clay had worked all morning. As they bumped past the open gate, Annie saw Clay in the distance driving a tractor with a disk attached. Jase followed pulling a machine that broadcast seed.

Steering her car along the fence line until she reached a group of trees, Annie pressed the horn several times, then climbed out.

"Unpack our lunch, girls," she called to Tara and Rachel. "I'll stop them when they make this round."

Stepping out into the field, Annie waited, smiling

as Clay neared. "Hey!" she called, waving a hand over her head. "How about some lunch?"

Clay slowed, grinning, and pulled the lever to raise the blades of the disk. "Don't have to ask me twice."

While he shut off the tractor's engine and climbed down, Annie stepped farther out into the field to stop Jase. She kept her smile in place when she saw his scowl. Fitting her hands at the sides of her mouth to be heard over his tractor's engine, she yelled, "We brought your lunch!"

He slowed, then stopped, his scowl deepening. "Clay was supposed to go to the house and get it."

Pushing her smile higher, Annie replied, "I know, but we thought a picnic might be fun." Before he could argue, she turned and headed back for the trees and the quilt the girls had spread out.

"How about some lemonade, Clay?" she asked and filled a plastic cup from the thermos she'd brought along.

He accepted the cup with a grin. "Thanks, Annie." He plopped down on the quilt and dug around in the basket. "What did you make for us? I'm starving."

Tara slapped his hand away. "Sandwiches, you moron, and keep your skanky hands off. You're dirty."

Clay sat back, still grinning, seemingly willing to let his twin sister wait on him. "What kind?"

"Tuna, pimento cheese or turkey," Tara said, assuming the position of hostess. "Which would you like?"

"All of 'em."

Tara shot him a frown. "Pig."

Clay's grin spread wider. "I'm not a pig. I'm a workin' man and workin' men have big appetites."

Annie laughed, unaffected by the twins' bickering, recognizing it as the harmless teasing that siblings exchanged.

"I want pimento cheese," Rachel piped in as she dropped down to her knees on the quilt.

Tara filled a plate and passed it to her brother, then arranged another for Rachel. "Annie?" she asked. "What about you?"

"Turkey, please," Annie replied, pleased to see that Tara's sullen expression was gone and she was actually smiling. "And one of those pickles, too," she added. She glanced up as Jase approached. "What kind of sandwich would you like, Jase?"

"What are my choices?" he grumbled.

Annie repeated the selections.

"Tuna," he said, and dropped down on the far end of the quilt, as far away from the others as he could possibly get.

Tara quickly arranged several sandwiches on a plate and passed it to her father.

He accepted it without looking up or acknowledging the gesture. Seeing the disappointment on Tara's face, Annie quickly offered, "The girls helped make the sandwiches."

Jase grunted a response and took a bite, while Clay faked a choking sound. "Tara helped cook?" He clutched his stomach dramatically. "I've been poisoned!"

Pursing her lips, Tara slugged him on the arm and Clay fell over as if she'd delivered a knockout punch. Rachel laughed and fell on top of her brother and began tickling him. Tara joined in and, with the two girls teaming up, they quickly pinned their brother to the ground, laughing at the advantage they'd gained.

"You kids settle down," Jase snapped. He waved an impatient hand. "And hurry up and eat. Clay and I have work to do."

The wrestling match came to a abrupt stop and Tara sat up, the laughter in her eyes dying as she looked over at her father. Slowly she shifted off Clay and picked up her plate. Rising, she carried it to the trunk of Annie's car and pitched it into the paper sack they'd brought to collect their garbage, then climbed into the front seat and slammed the door behind her.

Annie watched Tara, her heart sinking.

Later that night, after the children had gone to bed, Annie waited for Jase to return to the house, hoping to talk to him about the picnic and explain to him how he'd spoiled a perfectly wonderful outing and how deeply he'd disappointed his children by doing so.

She watched for him from the back porch, perched on the first step, dressed in her nightgown and robe, her arms hugged around her knees. The night was blessedly cool, a respite from the unseasonably hot afternoon, and Annie tipped up her chin to peer at the sky. Stars blinked overhead, scattered across a field of blue-black velvet, and a sickle-shaped moon hung low in the sky.

In the distance she could hear the low call of cattle and closer the hum of insects darting in and out of the glow of the security light near the barn. Though she'd spent her entire life in the city surrounded by people, noise and lights, she sighed contentedly, surprised to discover that she found the pastoral setting much more appealing.

Her sense of contentment ended with Jase's approach. Though he remained in shadows as he strode for the house, she could tell by the squareness of his shoulders, the deliberateness of his stride, that his mood hadn't improved since the picnic that afternoon. As he neared, she hugged her arms tighter around her knees, dreading the confrontation even as awareness fluttered to life low in her belly.

"What are you doing out here?"

Though his tone was anything but friendly, Annie forced a smile. "Waiting for you."

He snorted as he passed by her, climbing the steps. "It's late. I'm going to bed."

She caught the leg of his jeans, stopping him. "Sit down for a minute. Please?" she added, looking up at him. "I need to talk to you."

He hesitated a moment, then, heaving a sigh, swung around and dropped down on the step beside her. He dragged off his hat, swiped an arm across his forehead, then settled the hat back over his head. "Make it fast. I'm tired."

"I'm sure you are. You've been at it since dawn this morning."

"Yeah, well," he replied dryly, "there's always work to be done on a ranch."

"Yes, I'm sure there is." She caught the fabric of her robe over her knees and pleated it between her fingers, unsure how to broach the subject of his behavior. "About the picnic this afternoon," she began.

He snorted and pushed to his feet. "I don't have time for this."

She caught the leg of his jeans again, stopping him. "Please hear me out."

Though she could tell by the tension he kept on the fabric that he wanted to avoid this conversation, he finally dropped back down and dragged off his hat, balancing it over his knee. "Say what you've got to say and get it over with."

"Are you aware that you hurt Tara's feelings this afternoon?"

He whipped his head around. "How the hell did I do that? I ate with y'all, didn't I?"

"Yes, but when I told you that the girls helped make your lunch, you just grunted."

He huffed a disgusted breath. "What was I supposed to do? Break out in song?"

"No," she replied, ignoring his sarcasm. "But you might have offered them a compliment or, at the very least, said thank you."

"Did *they* thank me for providing the food they prepared?" he returned defensively. "Did *they* do anything to help earn the money to buy that food?"

"Jase, they are children."

"So was I, once upon a time, but I worked right alongside my daddy on this ranch from the time I was six years old. Didn't seem to hurt me any."

"I think it did."

He turned his head to glare at her.

"You obviously never learned how to play."

He snorted and would have risen, but Annie stopped him by placing a hand on his arm. "Let them be children, Jase. They'll be forced to become adults soon enough.''

''They'll grow up lazy.''

''No,'' she argued, ''they'll grow up to be happy and well-adjusted adults.''

''Lazy,'' he repeated.

''Would you rather they be workaholics, like you?'' she asked in frustration.

His eyes narrowed and darkened. ''As long as there's work to be done, I'll do it.''

Knowing that she'd angered him, that she was growing angry herself, she took a deep breath, forcing herself to calm down. ''You said yourself that there is *always* work to be done on a ranch,'' she reminded him pointedly. ''If you don't take time for yourself, for your family, put off some of the work for another day, another time, you're going to kill yourself or, at the very least, alienate your children and wind up a lonely and bitter old man.''

He stared at her for a long moment, his lips thinning, his eyes narrowing dangerously. ''Are you through?''

She released his arm, sure that she'd failed in getting her point across to him. ''Yes. I'm through.''

''Good,'' he said, rising. '''Cause I'm through listening.''

Annie glanced at the clock, then snatched the platter of fried chicken from the table and marched to the refrigerator.

''The coward,'' she muttered as she shoved the platter inside. Not coming in for lunch, and after she'd prepared a perfectly good meal for him, too. She knew it was Jase's way of avoiding talking to her, an immature and childish act, in her opinion. Not that she was foolish enough to believe that talking to him was going to change anything. She might only be a *girl,* as he liked to refer to her, but she wasn't a fool.

She'd known when she'd persuaded him to let her stay on as the children's nanny that she had her work cut out for her, the least of which was dealing with a rebellious teen. What Tara needed was love, attention and a firm, guiding hand, all of which Annie was more than willing to provide for the teenager. But Tara also needed her father, and convincing Jase to be more attentive, to express his love more openly to his daughter, as well as his other two children…well, that placed Annie right smack in the middle between father and daughter, an uncomfortable place to be, she was fast coming to realize.

Feeling the frustration building, she crossed to the sink, her gaze going instinctively to the window and the barn beyond where Jase had worked all morning. At breakfast, he'd ignored Annie, wolfed down his meal and left the house before the children even came downstairs for the day, choosing to hide out in the barn rather than deal with them or her.

Which left Annie to wonder if anything she'd said the night before had penetrated that thick skull of his. His children needed him. All of them, but especially Tara.

She caught a movement inside the barn and stilled, watching as Jase stepped out into the sunlight, shirt-less and stooped beneath a heavy sack of feed he carried on one shoulder. Perspiration gleamed on his arms and chest and dripped from his chin as he strained to heave the sack onto the bed of the truck. She watched the muscles on his arms and back ripple at the effort...and swallowed hard, forced to admit that she needed Jase, too. Not in the same way as his children, but she definitely needed him.

No, she corrected, feeling the swell of longing rise as she watched him disappear inside the barn again. She *wanted* him, which was a totally different emotion from need. Need was a requirement, something vital to one's well-being, whereas want was purely selfish, and, in this case, purely physical, a desire of the flesh. A desire that he seemed to share, but one he seemed intent to deny as diligently as he fought to maintain an emotional distance from his children.

Her eyes sharpened, then narrowed as he stepped from the barn burdened beneath another sack of feed. What if she managed to somehow break down his resistance? she wondered. What if she were able to coax some of that emotion from him? The kind of emotion she'd witnessed and experienced firsthand when he'd kissed her that afternoon in the barn? Would it free him up to express more of his emotions and feelings? The ones he withheld from his children?

Could she teach him how to play?

Convinced that her theory was at least worth a try, she hurried to the refrigerator and pulled out the plate of fried chicken she'd prepared for their lunch.

Jase tossed the last sack of feed onto the bed of his truck, then lifted his hat and dragged an arm across his forehead, wiping away the sweat that dripped into his eyes, before settling the hat wearily back over his head. With a baleful glance at the sun and the unseasonable heat it was casting, he headed for the driver's side of his truck and climbed inside.

He revved the engine, cranked up the air conditioner a notch, then let out the clutch. The truck hadn't rolled forward more than a couple of feet when he heard a shout from behind. He glanced over his shoulder and saw Annie jogging toward him, jostling a basket in one hand, while waving the other frantically over her head.

Though tempted to make her eat his dust, he stomped on the brake, then leaned across the seat to roll down the passenger window. "What do you want?" he asked impatiently as she came to a stop beside the door.

"Lunch," she replied breathlessly, then smiled and lifted the basket for him to see. Before he could tell her that he wasn't hungry, she was climbing into the cab and forcing him back onto his seat with the basket she shoved onto the console between them. "Where are you headed?" she asked, clipping her seat belt into place.

"To put out some feed in the back pasture." He leaned across her and pushed open the door. "I'm sure you've got better things to do than ride along."

She smiled and pulled the door closed again. "No, actually, I don't." She dipped her head down to peer up at the sun as she rolled up the window. "It's a perfect day for a picnic, don't you think?"

"Picnic?" he repeated. "Again?"

"The one Saturday was such a flop that I thought you might need a little practice to get the hang of it."

"Look. I really don't have time for—"

"Cool," she said, distracting him by leaning to fiddle with the eight ball Clay had attached to the head of the stick shift. "Can I drive?" she asked, glancing up at him. "I haven't driven a standard transmission in years."

And if he had his way, Jase thought irritably, it would be another couple of years before she had the pleasure again. Scowling, he shoved her hand away and shifted into first with a grinding of gears. "No," he informed her with a little more force than necessary, then stomped on the accelerator.

The truck shot forward, throwing Annie back against her seat. She laughed gaily, kicked off her sandals and lifted her feet to prop them on the dash.

With her feet up in the air, Jase couldn't help noticing her toenails and the putrid shade of blue she insisted on polishing them. He waved a disgusted hand. "Why the hell do you paint your toenails that color?"

She wiggled her toes, admiring her polish. "It's called Wild Blue Yonder. Like it?"

"No." He shifted his gaze to glare at the road ahead. "Makes me sick to my stomach every time I look at it."

She stole a glance at him, her tongue tucked against the inside of her cheek. "Really? Then why do you keep looking?"

"Who could help but notice," he shot back angrily, "with you running around barefoot all the time."

She wiggled her toes, infuriating him further by drawing his gaze to her feet again, and the long stretch of bare, tanned legs. "But I like going barefoot. Don't you?"

"Wouldn't know," he replied, determined to ignore her. "Never done it."

She leaned to give his arm a playful punch. "Oh, come on. Surely you must have gone barefoot when you were a kid?"

He hunched his shoulder and drew his arm across his chest, avoiding her touch. "Can't remember that far back."

She settled back against the seat, seemingly unoffended. "That's too bad, because it's fun. And sensual," she added with a wicked grin and wiggled her toes again. "There's nothing quite like walking barefoot through grass when it's covered with early-morning dew. Or walking along a beach and feeling the wet sand ooze between your toes. You should try it sometime."

He braked to a fast stop and killed the engine. "I think I'll pass," he muttered dryly.

She sat up, dropping her feet to the floorboard, to peer through the windshield. "Are we there?"

"Yeah." He pushed open his door and hopped to the ground. The sound of the passenger door slamming echoed that of his. He glanced across the bed of the truck, frowning. "What are you doing?"

She lifted a hand to shade her eyes. "Looking for a spot for our picnic. Oh!" she cried, pointing. "Is that a creek over there by those trees?"

He followed the line of her finger. "If you want to call it that." He reached into the back of the truck and dragged a sack to the end of the tailgate. "More often than not, its nothing but a dry wash."

"But with all the rain we've had this winter, I'll bet there's water running in it now."

He lifted the bag of feed, straining as he hefted it to his shoulder. "Probably. Won't last long, though. In another couple of weeks it'll be dry as a bone."

With a huff of breath, she turned and planted a fist on her hip. "You are undoubtably the most negative person I've ever met in my life."

He crossed to a trough and dumped the bag inside. "I'm a realist," he replied and rammed a hand into his pocket, fishing out his pocket knife. "Easier to face reality head on, than try to avoid it by trying to turn everything into some kind of damn fairy tale."

Leading with her chin, she turned for the creek. "But not nearly as much fun," she replied airily, swinging the basket at her side.

He stared after her a moment, then dropped his gaze and stabbed the knife into the bag, ripping it open. "Damn fool *girl*," he muttered.

"I heard that!" she called over her shoulder.

He snapped up his head and was surprised to see that she'd almost reached the stand of trees that grew alongside the creek. Realizing that she hadn't bothered to put on her shoes, he shook his head as he watched her pick her way carefully through the tall weeds. "Better watch out for—" He winced when he heard her cry of alarm. "Stickers," he finished too late. He dumped the feed into the trough, tossed the empty bag into the back of the truck, then started after her. "You okay?" he called.

"No," she wailed. "I've got a sticker in my foot. Ouch!" she cried, then added miserably, "Make that both feet."

Standing with her toes pointed at the sky and her heels dug into the ground, she created a comical picture. As hard as he tried, Jase couldn't stop the smug smile that spread across his face.

"Don't you dare say 'I told you so,'" she warned as he drew near.

He lifted his hands in surrender. "Wouldn't dream of it, although I do feel obligated to point out that this is a prime example of one of the many dangers of going barefoot, which, I might add, I've been wise to avoid over the years."

"That's the same as saying 'I told you so,'" she grumbled, then squealed when he stooped and hooked an arm behind her knees. "What are you doing!" she cried as he swung her up against his chest.

"Carrying you."

"But our lunch," she began, stretching a hand toward the basket. She shrieked, flinging her arms around his neck, when he leaned forward, dipping her over it.

"Grab a hold," he ordered.

Pursing her lips, she shot him a frown, then snatched the basket's handle, clinging to it as well as his neck when he straightened.

She brightened when he headed for the creek and not back to his truck. "Does this mean we're going to have our picnic now?"

He plopped her down on a large rock beside the slow-moving creek and squatted down, catching her ankle and drawing her foot up to study it. "Soon as I dig these stickers out."

"Dig?" she repeated, her smile melting. "With what?"

He propped her foot on his knee while he worked his knife from his pocket. "This."

Her eyes widened when he flipped the knife open and the sun's rays struck a lethal-looking blade. Swallowing hard, she inched her foot back toward her hip. "But won't that hurt?"

"Depends on your tolerance for pain."

"It's low," she was quick to inform him, then caught her lip between her teeth and added nervously, "Really low."

He eased her foot back over his knee. "If you've got a weak stomach, you might want to look the other way."

"No," she replied, not trusting him. "I'll watch."

He lifted a shoulder and curled his fingers around her foot, angling it for better access. "Your call."

In spite of her intention to watch the proceedings, Annie squeezed her eyes shut, every muscle in her body tensing in dread as she waited for the painful dig of the knife.

"You might want to breathe," he suggested.

She flipped open her eyes to find him watching her, his gray eyes filled with amusement. "Oh," she murmured in embarrassment, then leaned to peer more closely at him, noticing the changes a smile made to his face. "You really should smile more often," she said without thinking.

He snorted a laugh and shifted his gaze to her foot. "Why?"

"Because...well, just because," she replied, flustered.

"Now *there's* a reason," he replied dryly as he probed the blade against the tender skin of her arch.

"Ouch!" she cried, jerking her foot from his hand.

"Sissy," he teased and held up the sticker for her inspection.

She rubbed her sore foot. "Easy for you to say."

He chuckled and reached to catch her other ankle. "Want me to kiss it and make it better?"

"And chance an infection?"

"Funny," he said and lifted the knife again.

"Yeah," she said, tensing for the probe of the blade. "About as funny as you." Determined not to make a sound, she was surprised when he held up the second sticker. "Hey!" she cried. "I didn't feel a thing that time."

"I could try again," he offered.

"No," she replied, laughing, pleased to discover that he had a sense of humor. "I think I'll quit while I'm ahead. Otherwise, you might decide to amputate."

Still holding her foot, he glanced up, his forehead creasing as he peered at her, the teasing fading from his eyes. "Do you really think I would purposely hurt you?"

She snorted a laugh and relaxed back against the rock, supporting herself with her elbows. "I think you'd do most anything to get me out of your house."

He frowned and glanced down at her foot, stroking his thumb thoughtfully along her arch. "You're young," he said, as if he felt he needed to justify his less-than-friendly treatment of her.

She rolled her eyes. "Oh, give it up, would you? It isn't my age that bothers you."

"No. But it's reason enough."

"For you, maybe."

"And it should be for you, as well."

"Look," she said patiently. "I'm an adult. I know how to take care of myself. And I don't need you, or anybody else trying to do the job for me. So why don't we just agree to disagree on the subject of my maturity level and go on from here?"

Jase stroked his thumb along her arch, from toe to heel and back again, his gaze narrowed thoughtfully on hers, wondering if she realized how far over her head she was when it came to dealing with a man as calloused as him. Thinking a lesson might be in order, he said, "All right. Sounds fair enough to me."

She sank back on her elbows. "By the way," she said and offered him a grudging smile. "Thanks for the massage. You've got good hands."

Frowning, he glanced down at her foot, unaware that he still held it, then looked back up at her, shaking his head as a slow smile chipped at one corner of his mouth. "You're welcome, though I'd have thought it would tickle to have your foot rubbed."

"Nope, but then I'm not ticklish. Are you?"

"A man never reveals his weaknesses."

"Which means you *are* ticklish."

"I didn't say that."

"You didn't have to." She sat up abruptly. "Take off your boots."

Startled, he barked a laugh. "Why?"

"Just take off your boots."

"I beg your pardon, ma'am," he said, feigning indignance, "but I'm not that kind of man."

She dropped back down to her elbows and smiled smugly. "You're ticklish, all right."

"It isn't wise to question a man's honesty when he's holding your foot."

"Why?"

He drew her toes to his mouth. "Because he might be tempted to take a bite."

Tensing, she gave her foot a tug, trying to free it, but he merely tightened his grip.

"You wouldn't dare," she warned, narrowing an eye at him.

"Wouldn't I?" His gaze on hers, he opened his mouth. But instead of biting her toe, he blew a long breath of moist, warm air along the arch of her foot. He bit back a smile when her leg jerked reflexively. "I thought you said you weren't ticklish?"

"I'm not."

"Then why'd you jump?"

"It was instinctive," she replied defensively. "An involuntary reaction to stimuli."

He smoothed his hand over her heel and up her calf, raising gooseflesh on her skin. "Maybe you better explain that in layman's terms," he suggested and drew her leg over his thigh as he shifted to sit on the rock beside her.

She stared up at him as he shaped his fingers around her calf and began to knead the muscle there. "Okay," she said, sounding a little breathless. "You're turning me on."

Five

Jase arched a brow, surprised by her bluntness. "I am?"

"Yeah," she said, her gaze shifting to his mouth as he leaned closer.

"And what do you think we should we do about that?"

She slicked her lips. "I don't know. What do you want to do?"

He puckered his mouth thoughtfully as if considering. "I suppose I could kiss you."

"Yeah," she said, releasing her breath on a sigh. "I guess you could."

"But that might be inviting trouble."

"For who?"

"Me. You," he added, his voice growing husky.

She slicked her lips again. "I'm willing to chance it, if you are."

"I don't know," he murmured. "I—"

But before he could voice his doubts, she lifted her head and pressed her mouth to his.

Though he fully intended to teach her a lesson, common sense told Jase to keep things light, to end things before they went too far. But he quickly discovered he couldn't. Really didn't want to even try. Their previous kiss had haunted his dreams at night and distracted him from his work during the day. He'd told himself that he'd only imagined the sweetness of her lips, that the years of deprivation had embellished his memories of her sensual response.

Anxious to prove his assumptions correct, he probed his tongue against the crease of her lips, gained entry, then groaned as her flavor poured through him, hot and enticing, sweet and cloying, just as he'd remembered…and feared. Her tongue swept over his, and he shoved aside all reason, giving in to the stronger need to explore.

Just one touch, he promised himself and slipped a hand between them. He cupped a breast, molding his palm around its shape, and she bowed her spine, arching instinctively toward the pressure of his hand.

With a groan, he rolled to his back, pulled her over him, and took the kiss deeper. The rock's jagged surface dug into his back, but he welcomed the pain for the greater reward of her weight, the softness of her body stretched along the length of his.

"You're trouble," he murmured, withdrawing far enough to nip at her lower lip. "I knew you'd be trouble."

"Yeah," she said, sighing, then shifted to a more comfortable position on his chest and grinned. "But ain't it fun?"

He chuckled, then grunted, the breath whooshing out of him as she planted her hands against his chest and pushed to her feet. She grabbed his boot and pulled. "Hey!" he cried, propping himself up on his elbows. "What do you think you're doing?"

The boot gave way and she stumbled back a step, then grinned and tossed it to the ground before reaching for the other. "Returning the favor."

He curled his toes inside the remaining boot, thwarting her efforts to remove it. "What favor?"

"The massage."

He leaned to swat at her hands. "I don't want you massaging my feet."

She arched a brow, biting back a smile. "Why? Are you ticklish?"

He scowled when, in spite of his efforts to keep it on, his boot slipped over his heel. "No, I'm not ticklish."

"Good, because you're getting a massage." She dropped the boot and picked up his foot. Slipping her hands inside the leg of his jeans, she smoothed her palms up his calf until her fingertips reached the elasticized band of his sock. A shiver chased up his spine and she smiled knowingly as she slowly stripped the sock down his leg and off the end of his toes.

She sank down to the ground at the base of the rock and drew his foot onto her lap. "There's an art to giving a good foot massage, you know," she said, sounding a little too pleased with herself.

Heat crawled up his neck as she drew her hands

from ankle to toe, her fingers drifting over the dark hair that dusted his instep, and between the joints of each toe. The contrast between his big, ugly foot and the graceful, slender fingers that cradled it was humbling, but no more so than having Annie sitting at his feet like a some kind of Grecian handmaiden. "No," he said, trying his best to ignore the sensual scrape of her nails along the bottom of his foot. "I didn't know."

"There is. I've studied a little about reflexology." She curled her fingers and dug her knuckles deeply into his arch, making every muscle in his body go limp as a wet rag. "There are pressure points on your foot that are tied to other parts of your body. For example," she said positioning her fingertips on the ball of his foot just below his little toe. "This area is connected to your shoulder. When I press here," she said, placing added stress on the spot, "you should be able to feel it in your shoulder. Do you?"

Jase felt something all right, but it sure as hell wasn't in his shoulder. "Yeah," he said, thinking it best not to tell her exactly *where* he felt the response.

She smiled, seeming satisfied, and resumed the massage. "The human body is a complex system of nerve and muscle, with everything connecting and responding to different stimuli."

Stimuli. There was that word again, he thought, frowning at her use of it. He wondered if she was purposely trying to turn him on, as she'd claimed he had her with his foot massage. He shifted his gaze to hers, expecting to find a coyness in her expression, or at the very least, a sly smugness. But he found only innocence in the depths of the green eyes that met his.

She smiled and curled her fingers around his foot, shaking it gently. "Relax," she scolded gently. "If you don't, you won't be able to enjoy the massage."

"I'm relaxed," he argued, though every muscle in his body felt as if it was caught in a vise and twisted tight.

She laughed and reached to pull off his other sock. "Yeah, and I can sing like Madonna." She stood and tossed his sock down to join his boots, then reached for his hand. "Come on," she said and gave him a tug, pulling him to his feet.

"Where are we going?" he asked as he high-stepped behind her, wincing as stones dug into his tender feet.

"Wading."

He stopped abruptly, drawing her up short, as well. "Uh-uh."

She gave his hand a tug, laughing. "Uh-huh."

"Uh-uh," he repeated more adamantly and tore his hand from her grasp.

Frowning, she propped her hands on her hips. "Why not?"

He jerked his chin toward the water. "No telling what's lying on the bottom of that creek."

"Chicken," she chided and turned for the bank.

"If you cut your foot or stub a toe," he called after her, "don't come crying to me."

"I won't." She waded out a few feet and shivered deliciously as the cool water struck her warm skin and lapped around her knees. She turned, smiling, and gestured for him to join her. "Come on in. The water feels wonderful."

He folded his arms stubbornly across his chest. "No thanks. I think I'll pass."

She lifted a shoulder and waded deeper, until the water reached the hem of her shorts. Laughing, she opened her arms wide, dropped her head back and spun in a slow circle.

"Watch out for rocks," he warned.

She drew her hair up on top of her head and strode farther out. "Worrywart," she scolded, laughing. Water rushed around her shoulders and filled her shirt, making it balloon out from her body.

Jase strained to keep an eye on her. "Annie! Get back over here before you drown."

She turned and grinned mischievously. "If you want me, you'll have to come and get me."

Jase took a step toward the water, then stopped. "Dammit! Get over here."

Annie's smile slowly gave way to incredulity as she saw the real fear in his eyes. "You can't swim, can you?"

"Who said anything about swimming?" he snapped. "I just want you out of that water before you hurt yourself."

Realizing that his concern for her was sincere, Annie started back for the bank. "I'm sorry," she said contritely. "I didn't intend to frighten—" Her eyes flipped wide as her foot slipped on a moss-covered rock and shot out from under her. She shrieked, dropping her hands from her hair in an effort to catch herself, but failed.

Jase was hip deep in the creek before her head

slipped completely beneath the water. His heart in his throat, he charged forward, fighting his way against the slow-moving current. When he reached the spot where he'd seen her go under, he dived his hands down into the water and fished frantically around. Not finding her, he glanced around and swore ripely when he saw her head bob to the surface a good ten feet downstream. She stood and swept her wet hair back from her face, sputtering water and laughing.

"You did that on purpose," he accused.

"I didn't," she said, still laughing.

"You damn sure did."

Annie sobered at the thunderous look on his face and started carefully making her way back toward him. "No. I swear. My foot slipped. Really."

"I told you not to go into the water, that you might get hurt."

She stopped, blinking water from her eyes as she stared up at him, stunned by the intensity of his anger. "But I'm not hurt. I just lost my footing."

"Well, you might have been hurt."

She laid a hand on his arm. "But I'm not," she insisted gently, hoping to reassure him.

With a growl, he shook free of her touch, started to turn away, then whirled back around and snatched her up into his arms. His mouth came down hard on hers, forcing her head back and stealing her breath. She tasted the fear on his lips, the anger, the desperate dig of his fingers into her back. He cared for her, she realized with a suddenness that had her heart slamming against her ribs. As hard as he tried to pretend otherwise, he truly cared what happened to her. Awed by the realization, she slowly wrapped her arms around his neck and drew his face closer to hers.

She was only slightly aware of his movements as he dipped to catch her beneath the knees. But as he lifted her to his chest and started for the bank, she smiled against his lips. "My hero," she murmured.

He jerked his head back and frowned down at her. "Don't kid yourself," he muttered and set her down on her feet on the bank.

Smiling, she caught her hair up in her hands and sank down on the soft grass at the edge of the bank as she twisted her wet hair up into a knot on her head. "And all this time I thought you were a mean old grizzly, when you're nothing but a big teddy bear."

He dropped down beside her and picked up a stick. "You must've taken in more water than I realized," he grumbled, dragging the stick through the wet sand and avoiding her gaze. "Made your brain soggy."

She bumped a shoulder against his, her smile widening at the blush that stained his cheeks. "Cut the macho act, wise guy. You might have fooled me in the past, but not any longer."

"Don't."

She laughed and caught the hem of her shirt between her hands, wringing the excess water from it. "Don't what?"

He dropped his gaze to the front of her shirt, then slowly brought it back to her face. Her smile slowly faded at the heat she saw in his eyes.

"Don't make the mistake of thinking I'm a nice guy," he warned. "I'm not."

Nerves danced to life beneath her skin as she

watched his face draw nearer. "I've never really cared for overly nice men," she said breathlessly.

"Don't say I didn't warn you," he said just before he crushed his mouth over hers. He forced her back against the soft grass and followed her down, pressing his bare chest against her damp one. Rolling, he pulled her over him.

He stiffened, groaning, when her pelvis bumped against his arousal. At the contact, he withdrew slightly and their gazes met with an awareness that had heat arcing between them. Suddenly the air seemed too thick to breathe.

Jase reached for her and captured her face between his palms, stunned by the intensity of the desire that swelled within him. Searching her gaze, he smoothed his thumbs beneath her lower lashes and watched the passion rise on her face, the heat spread to glaze her eyes. Slowly he lifted his head and claimed her mouth with his again.

He inhaled deeply as he swept his lips over hers, as he drank greedily of her essence. The golden warmth of sunshine, the sweet scent of the grass crushed beneath him and tangled in her damp hair. He heard her soft whimper, felt the claw of her fingers against his bare flesh, and his need for her sharpened, turned impatient. He rolled again, placing her on her back against the ground and moved to straddle her, his chest heaving with each drawn breath as he gazed down at her. "I want to touch you," he whispered and caught the hem of her wet shirt, shoving it up and baring her stomach. "And taste you," he said and dipped his head to press his mouth over the flat plane of her abdomen.

"Yes," she gasped, filling her hands with his hair. "Oh my, yes," she moaned as he dragged his lips up her rib cage. She sucked in a breath, arching, when he closed his mouth over her breast.

He swept his tongue across the budded nipple and groaned at the rich textures he found there, the added flavors.

Knowing he had to have her, he cupped a hand around her breast and slowly pulled it from his mouth. "I want to make love with you," he said, looking up at her.

Without a word, without a second's hesitation, she opened her arms in silent invitation.

He sank against her chest and dropped his mouth over hers, stabbing his tongue between her lips as he reached for the waist of her shorts. "Are you protected?" he asked, his voice as rusty as he feared was his technique.

When she tensed, he froze, then slowly drew back to look at her.

"Well...no," she said, her eyes wide as she stared at him. "Don't you have something?"

Groaning, Jase dropped his forehead against hers. "Not with me."

"Jase?"

He felt her fingers drawing small nervous circles on his back. "What?"

"I wrapped the fried chicken in plastic wrap. Maybe we could—"

In spite of his frustration, his disappointment, he found himself chuckling. Damn, but she was priceless. He rolled to his back and gathered her against his side. "I don't think plastic wrap would make a very effective form of birth control."

She pushed her mouth out into a pout. "Darn. And just when things were really heating up."

Laughing, he hugged her to his side. "It'll keep."

She lifted her head from his chest to peer up at him, her eyes filled with hope. "Later, then?"

"Yeah," he promised as he tucked her head beneath his chin. "Later."

Though it was pushing midnight, Jase stood at his bedroom window, a hand braced high on the molding. He stared blindly out at the night, waiting... wondering. Would Annie come to him? Though his body thrummed with need, and had since leaving her, he hoped she wouldn't. He feared, if she did, he wouldn't be able to resist her.

Later, he remembered telling her, and curled his hand into a fist against the wood, regretting the promise he'd made. What had come over him? he asked himself. He hadn't intended to get physically involved with her. Knew it would be a big mistake.

Annie, he reflected miserably. *She* was what had come over him. With that firm little body of hers. Those laughing green eyes. That sassy mouth. She'd teased him into remembering the pleasures a man could share with a woman, bewitched him into forgetting the hurt that would be inevitable if he allowed anyone to get too close. For the length of an afternoon, he'd let go of the memories, the fears, and had been ready to take advantage of what she freely offered.

The lack of a condom was all that had saved him.

He heard the door open softly behind him and tensed, knowing it was Annie who had entered his room. Her scent reached him first, that subtle, feminine fragrance that teased his senses every time she was near. He felt the warmth of her hand on the small of his back, her touch light and reassuring on his bare skin. Then she was standing at his side, looking up at him, and he could feel the heat of her gaze on his cheek.

''Jase?''

He closed his eyes at the huskiness in her voice, praying for the strength to send her back to her room. But when he opened his eyes and looked down at her, saw the heat, the expectancy in her wide green eyes, he knew the prayer was wasted. There was no way in hell he could send her away. Not now.

Knowing this, he dropped his arm from the window. He crossed to the bedside table, opened the drawer and pulled out a gold packet. He nudged the drawer closed with a knuckle and stood there a moment, palming the gold packet, then angled his head to peer at her across the shadowed room. ''You sure you want to go through with this?''

She hugged her arms around her middle as if suddenly chilled. ''Do you?''

He stared at her a moment, then slowly nodded his head. ''Yeah, though I have a feeling we're both going to regret it.''

She took a hesitant step toward him. ''Why? We're both consenting adults. We know what we're doing.''

He snorted a rueful laugh and sank down on the side of the bed. ''Do we?'' Leaning forward, he braced his forearms on his thighs and shook his head, staring at the condom he held. "I'm not so sure."

Wondering at the cause for his hesitancy, Annie crossed to the bed and sat down beside him. "Are you not ready for another physical relationship? I mean...well...if you feel guilty because of your wife—"

He shook his head. "No. It isn't that." He inhaled deeply, then released the breath with a weary sigh and angled his head to look over at her. "But you hit the nail on the head when you said physical. That's all I'm looking for in a relationship. Just the physical. If you understand that, then we shouldn't have any problems."

Annie's heart broke a little as the moon chased the shadows from his face, revealing the bleakness of his expression. Though she hadn't expected anything more than a no-strings-attached relationship with him, it saddened her to realize that he thought he could exclude feeling and emotion from their affair, as well. To her, lovemaking was a form of expression, an act that demanded, in and of itself, all the emotions that he stubbornly chose to deny. It stripped people down to their most elemental level, leaving them vulnerable and exposed to exquisite joy...or utter despair.

But perhaps he did know that, she realized slowly. Perhaps that's why he'd offered the warning when he'd placed the choice of making love with him in her hands. Maybe he was trying to spare her any hurt.

But what he didn't know was that she'd made her decision long before coming to his room. Maybe as early as that first morning when he'd stepped into the kitchen after his return home and found a new nanny there. And she'd done so fully aware of the pitfalls that might await her, willing to accept the dangers in exchange for any rewards that might be gained.

She smiled softly and laid her hand against his cheek. "No need to worry," she assured him, stroking a thumb along the high ridge of his cheekbone. "I understand."

He stared at her a moment as if he wasn't sure he'd heard her correctly, then reached up to cover her hand with his. She felt the tremble in his fingers as he drew her palm to his lips and pressed a kiss to its center. Tears filled her throat at the tenderness in the gesture, the kindness in it. Though he wanted to deny his emotions, they were there, she knew, just waiting to be set free.

She rose, her back to him, and caught the belt of her robe, tugged it loose, then slipped the garment from her shoulders and let it fall to pool around her feet. Gathering her nightgown in her hands, she turned to face him and slowly pulled it up and over her head, shaking out her hair as she dropped it behind her. As he moved his gaze down her body, she had to will her knees not to tremble at the hunger she saw reflected in his eyes. But when he returned his gaze to hers and reached to take her hand in his, drawing her to him, she stepped boldly and willingly between his spread knees.

He stared at her for a long moment, then dropped his gaze to their joined hands, watching his thumb's movement as he stroked it slowly across her knuckles. "It's been a long time," he said quietly. "This might be over before we even get started good."

"We've got all night."

Jase glanced up at her in surprise, then, seeing the amusement in her eyes, smiled ruefully. "Yeah, I guess we do at that." He let his gaze slide down to her mouth and his sex swelled uncomfortably within his jeans as he stared at her lips, remembering the feel of them heated and moving beneath his. More than his next breath, he wanted to tug her down on the bed and cover her mouth with his, thrust himself deep inside her with a fierceness and an urgency that equaled that of the need swelling inside him.

Realizing how wrong that would be, how selfish, he tore his gaze from her mouth, and glanced away, shaking his head. "This is awkward as hell," he muttered.

"Why?"

"I don't know," he said irritably. "It just is."

"Perhaps because it seems so calculated?" she suggested softly. "So premeditated?"

He scowled. "Yeah. Maybe." He pushed to his feet, tossing the gold packet to the bed, and brushed past her to pace across the room. He stopped in front of the window and stuffed his hands into the pockets of his jeans as he frowned out at the darkness.

He heard the whisper of her feet against the carpet as she crossed to him, and tensed as her arms wound around his waist from behind. He felt the moist softness of her lips against his spine as she pressed a kiss there, and closed his eyes, fighting the urge to turn and drag her into his arms.

"Look at me, Jase," she whispered. When he didn't respond, she added, "Please?"

Unable to ignore the entreaty in her voice, he inhaled deeply and turned within the circle of her arms, intending to send her back to her room before it was too late.

Before he could speak, she pressed a finger against his lips as if sensing his intent. "Empty your mind of everything. Pretend that we're a just a man and woman who are attracted to each other and meeting for the first time."

Shaking his head sadly, he lifted his hands and combed his fingers through her hair above her ears, then held his palms against her cheek. "If only it were that simple."

"Why can't it be?"

"Because it's been a long time," he said, his frustration returning right along with his need for her. "Dammit! I could hurt you."

She took a step closer, a tender smile trembling at her lips as she pressed her body against his. "You won't hurt me. You couldn't."

"You don't know what I'm capa—"

Before he could say more, she rose to the balls of her feet and covered his mouth with hers, smothering his argument. At the feel of her lips on his, he surrendered to the heat and desire he tasted there and, with a groan, pulled her hard against him. Capturing her face between his hands, he took possession of the kiss, drinking deeply, thirstily, greedily. Each new taste he encountered, each new texture he discovered, pushed the level of his need higher, making him forget his resolve to send her away, and he backed her toward the bed.

"Yes," she murmured as he hauled her hips roughly against his groin, bowing her back over the bed. He dragged his lips to her throat and forced her down, then followed, stretching his body out over hers.

"Oh, yes, there," she whispered when he found her breast with his mouth and closed his lips over its rosy center. He drew her deeply into his mouth, sweeping his tongue over her turgid nipple and she arched up hard against him.

"I want to touch you," she said as she fumbled feverishly for the snap of his jeans. Finding it and quickly releasing it, she dragged the zipper down.

He groaned when her knuckles chafed against his sex. "Slow," he ordered and rolled to his back, drawing her on top of him. "I want this to last."

Her face flushed, she pushed against his chest until she was sitting up. "It will," she promised and quickly divested him of his jeans. Moving to straddle him, she smiled coyly as she dragged a finger from the hollow of his throat down to his navel. "Remember? We've got all night."

He caught her finger before she could carry it farther. "Not if you keep this up."

She laughed and leaned to drop a kiss on his mouth. "Always thinking negatively," she teased.

Seduced by her smile, by the passion he was only just discovering in her, he drew her finger to his mouth. "No. I just know my limits." Keeping his gaze on hers, he drew her finger into his mouth and suckled, watching her eyes widen, hearing her breath catch in her throat.

He slowly drew her finger from between his lips and she released the breath on a ragged sigh. "Don't be so sure," she warned and rose to her knees. Finding the gold packet, she opened it and fitted the condom over the sensitive tip of his sex. He moaned as she smoothed it down his length with a frustrating and erotic slowness. Sliding her gaze to his, she shifted back over him, took him in her hand and, with a seductive smile, slowly guided him to her.

Jase flinched, gritting his teeth, as the tip of his sex met her slick opening, then groaned as she lowered herself and took him in. With his heart pounding wildly against his chest and heat pumping through his veins with the speed of a grass fire raging out of control, he reached for her, drawing her face down to his. "I want you," he murmured against her lips. "All of you," he warned, then set his jaw and thrust deeply.

He swallowed her startled cry of pleasure and held her hips against his as the velvet walls of her feminine canal clamped tightly around him. He clenched his teeth, struggling for control, stunned by the flood of emotion that swept through him. She was so open, so honest, he realized as he stared at her. With her feelings, her thoughts, her actions. She hid nothing. Held back nothing. She took with the same measure of enthusiasm with which she so unselfishly gave.

Her pleasure was obvious in the softness of her expression, in the satisfied purr that slipped past her parted lips, in the heat that flushed her cheeks and glazed her eyes. But he was aware, too, of her desire to please him in the fingers that stroked seductively down his chest, saw it in the soft, knowing smile that curved the corners of her mouth as she boldly met his gaze.

And in giving, in her desire to please him, she only made him want to please her more. Slowly he began to move within her, each stroke a testament of his awareness of her, of his determination to please her before he sought pleasure for himself.

Her breath quickened as she rode him, matching each of his thrusts with the rise and fall of hips that seemed to match perfectly with the fit of his, the rhythm that he set. He watched her eyes widen, her lips part on a strangled gasp for air, felt the painful dig of her fingers against his flesh as a second climax pulled at her.

''Again,'' he growled and thrust hard one last time against her, shooting her high and over the edge. She arched, her fingers opening over his chest, then clenching, and she dropped her head back with a low, guttural moan as he found his own release within her throbbing center.

Stunned by the intensity of her climax and weakened by the debilitating power of his own, he dragged her down to his chest and wrapped his arms around her, holding her against him. ''Annie,'' he murmured and buried his face in her hair, inhaling her sweetness. ''Oh, Annie,'' he said on a sigh as she snuggled closer, her purr of contentment vibrating against his chest.

With his heart pounding against hers and his sex growing soft inside her, he closed his eyes, sure that he'd never experienced anything like this in his life…and wondering if he'd survive it.

''Again,'' she whispered.

He flipped his eyes wide, then tucked his chin back to peer at her. ''You've got to be kidding.''

With a devilish smile, she rocked her hips slowly against his. ''Dead serious.''

Groaning, he dropped his head back to the pillow and closed his eyes. "No way."

"Way," she insisted and stretched to tease his lower lip with her teeth.

His response was immediate...and surprising. Feeling himself growing hard again, he hooked an arm around her waist and flipped her on to her back beneath him. "Witch," he growled. He nipped at the bow of her lip, then dipped his head lower to catch a nipple lightly between his teeth.

She arched, knotting her fingers in his hair. "Yeah, I know," she said, sounding pleased with herself, then dragged his face back to hers.

Six

Missing the warmth of the body that had curled against his throughout the night, Jase rolled to his side and flung out an arm, intending to draw Annie back to his side. When his hand met only cool sheets, he blinked open his eyes and swallowed back the moan of disappointment at discovering he was alone in his bed.

Sighing, he rolled to his back and stared at the ceiling, remembering the wild night of lovemaking, the passion he'd discovered in Annie, shared with her...but tensed when he heard pans clattering in the kitchen. He snapped his head around to peer at the alarm clock on the bedside table, then bolted to his feet, weaving drunkenly as he stared at the clock in dismay.

"Damn," he swore as he staggered to the bathroom. He couldn't remember the last time he'd slept this late.

Fifteen minutes later, he stepped into the kitchen, freshly showered and shaved.

Annie glanced up from the stove. ''Good morning,'' she said, warming him with a secret smile. ''Did you sleep well?''

Jase roamed his gaze down her body, noting each feminine curve and swell beneath her robe and remembering the feel of each beneath his hands. ''Like a rock,'' he said and grinned as he returned his gaze to hers. ''And you?''

''Never better.''

''I slept good, too, Daddy.''

Jase paled at the sound of his youngest daughter's voice and turned to find all three of his children sitting at the breakfast table, staring at him. Sure that they could see the guilt that stained his face, knew how he'd spent the previous night, he stammered, ''Uh… that's good, dumplin'.''

''Gee, Dad,'' Clay said, peering at his father curiously. ''You *never* sleep this late. Are you sick or something?''

''No. That is…I—'' Jase made the mistake of glancing at Annie, who quickly turned back to the stove, smothering a smile. Scowling, he crossed to the counter and grabbed his hat. ''I put in a hard day's work yesterday,'' he growled as he rammed the hat over his head and reached for the doorknob. ''Something you kids ought to try for a change,'' he added and slammed the door behind him.

''Yeah,'' Tara muttered resentfully, ''like we never do anything around here.''

"You *don't* do anything," Clay said, quick to come to his father's defense.

"And you do?" Tara shot back.

"That's enough," Annie warned from the stove.

Tara shoved back her chair. "Dude, I'm outta here," she muttered and stomped from the room.

With a sigh, Annie dropped the spatula and tugged off her apron. "Rachel, you and Clay finish your breakfast and get ready for school."

"Where are you going?" Clay asked as she headed for the door.

"To talk to Tara."

"What about?" Rachel asked.

"Eat your breakfast," Annie ordered, then hurried for the stairs. When she reached Tara's room, she found the teenager sitting before her vanity, smearing a dark mahogany lipstick over her lips.

"Planning on wearing that to school?" Annie asked as she moved to stand behind Tara and peer at the girl's reflection.

Tara met her gaze in the mirror. "What's it to you?" she asked spitefully.

Annie lifted a shoulder. "Just wondered." She plucked a tissue from a box and held it out to the girl. "Though something tells me your father wouldn't approve."

Tara's scowl deepened, but she snatched the tissue from Annie's hand and dragged it across her lips, wiping away the lipstick. "Like he approves of anything I do," she said bitterly.

Her heart going out to the girl, Annie picked up a brush from the vanity. "He cares for you," she said softly as she stroked the brush through Tara's long hair.

"Hey!" Tara cried, ducking from beneath Annie's hand. "What do you think you're doing?"

Annie drew the brush back and lifted a shoulder. "I was just thinking that you're hair would look nice styled away from your face. Like this," she explained and demonstrated by gathering a length of her own hair and twisting it in a rope toward her crown.

Tara rolled her eyes. "Yeah, like my hair would stay that way."

"Mine wouldn't either without clips. You can borrow some, if you like," Annie offered, then grabbed Tara's hand and gave it a tug. "But we'd better hurry, or you'll miss the bus."

Tara dug in her heels. "What kind of clips?"

"Rhinestones, sunflowers." Annie lifted a shoulder. "You name it, I've got it."

Though the teenager tried to maintain her sullen look, Annie saw the gleam of interest that sparked in her eyes.

"Okay," Tara said grudgingly and allowed Annie to lead her from her room. "So long as I get to pick."

Annie waited until the children had left for school, then dressed and went in search of Jase. She found him out beside the barn, working on a piece of equipment.

"Hey," she said softly, curling her fingers around his neck as she bent over his stooped frame. "What are you doing?"

He jumped, swearing, then tossed the wrench to the ground and rose. Scowling, he tugged a rag from his back pocket and wiped his hands, avoiding her gaze. "Working."

She bit back a smile. "I can see that. But that doesn't tell me what you're doing."

He waved a hand at the piece of machinery he'd been tinkering with. "I'm tightening the belts on the baler."

"Belts?" she repeated curiously and stooped to peer inside the machine.

His scowl deepening, he bumped his shoulder against hers, nudging her out of his way. "I don't have time to give a lesson in mechanics," he said, hunkering down in front of the machine again. "I've got work to do."

Arching a brow at his resentful tone, Annie took a step back. "I didn't expect one."

He strained to tighten the nut on the bolt. "Good," he ground out. "Because you aren't getting one."

"And I didn't expect to have my head bitten off, either."

He braced a hand against the baler and angled his chest, straining to reach deep inside the machine to test the belt's tension. "That's too damn bad."

Feeling the anger boil up inside her, Annie caught the collar of his shirt and gave him a jerk, making him lose his balance and sit down hard on the ground.

He was on his feet with his face shoved up to hers before she had a chance to regret the petty action.

"Listen to me, little *girl*," he growled and took a threatening step, forcing her back. "I've got work to do and I don't have time to play any of your silly little games."

Annie flattened her hands against his chest, stopping his forward movement. "Who are you really mad at? Me? Or yourself?"

His eyes narrowed and a nerve ticked at his temple. "Me," he growled and turned away, dragging the rag from his pocket again.

Annie dropped her hands and released a long, shaky breath. "Well, at least you aren't so blind that you can't see who is at fault here."

"I'm not blind to anything," he snapped. "Least of all your womanly wiles."

She arched a brow. "So now I'm a woman? A second ago, you were calling me a girl again."

He whipped his head around to glare at her, but Annie merely offered him a guileless smile in return.

With a huff, he looked away, bracing his hands low on his hips. After a moment, he dropped his chin to his chest, inhaled deeply, then puffed his cheeks as he slowly released the breath. "I'm sorry."

"I'm not."

He shot her a look over his shoulder. "Last time you said those words, I had just apologized for kissing you."

"Want to again?"

He stared at her a moment, then snorted a laugh. Tossing down the rag, he crossed to her. "Come here," he said, and tugged her against his chest. He wrapped his arms around her and buried his nose in her hair, slowly rocking her back and forth. "I was embarrassed," he admitted reluctantly.

"Because of the children?"

Frowning, he drew back and caught a lock of her hair to tuck behind her ear. "Yeah, the kids," he said, finally meeting her gaze.

"But they didn't know why you'd slept late."

"*I* did."

She laughed and wrapped her arms around his waist, rubbing her thumbs along his spine above his belt. "You shouldn't feel guilty," she scolded gently. "I doubt the children would suffer any emotional trauma if they were to discover their father was physically attracted to a woman. Not that I'm suggesting that we should openly flaunt our affair," she was quick to add. "But it might be healthy for them to see you interact with a woman."

He moaned and dropped his forehead to rest against hers. "Easy for you to say. They aren't your kids."

Annie felt a pang of regret at the reminder. "No," she said slowly, realizing how attached she'd become to Jase's children and how much she wished they were hers. "But I don't think I'd feel any differently if they were."

He shook his head and dropped his arms from around her. "I knew this was a mistake," he said, turning away.

Her heart froze in her chest. "What's a mistake?"

"This!" he cried and whirled to face her. "You and me. You're my kids' nanny, for God's sake! A good ten years or more younger than me. Hell!" he said, throwing up his hands. "There are probably laws against a man having sex with his employee."

"Yes, and they were designed to protect women whose employers tried to force them into granting sexual favors. But you didn't force me," she reminded him. "I entered into this relationship with you willingly and with my eyes wide-open, so you certainly can't blame yourself for seducing me."

"I don't," he shot back. "But that sure as hell doesn't mean I have to be fool enough to make the mistake of sleeping with you again."

Annie stumbled back a step, stunned by his anger, but even more so by his announcement that he intended to end their affair. She stared at him, praying that he would take it all back, that he'd realize he was overreacting. She searched for a crack in his stony expression, anything that would indicate regret for the angrily spouted threat...but found nothing but cold determination.

Left with nothing but her pride to sustain her, she turned for the house. "Fine," she said, telling herself the sound she heard wasn't her heart breaking. "And I'll certainly do my part to stay out of your way."

From the kitchen window, Annie watched the children emerge from the school bus. She quickly dabbed the dish towel at her eyes, not wanting them to know she'd been crying. She'd allowed herself a good, long pity party over the end of her relationship with Jase, but it was time now to set aside her sadness and put on a happy face. The children were home, and it was her job to take care of them, to add some sunshine to their lives. God knew they had enough to deal with without having to contend with a blubbering-feeling-sorry-for-herself nanny.

Glancing out the window again, she saw the sullen look on Tara's face as Clay passed his backpack to her, then watched Clay trudge toward the barn and his waiting chores. As she watched, something inside her snapped. She raced to the back door and flung it open. "Clay!" she shouted, waving a hand over her head.

He turned, frowning, to peer at her. "Yes, ma'am?"

The girls reached the door and she quickly herded them past her and into the house, then yelled, "Come here, please! I've got something I want you to do."

Clay glanced uneasily toward the barn, where he knew his father waited, then back at Annie. With a shrug, he headed for the house.

"What do you want Clay to do?" Rachel asked as Annie stepped inside the kitchen.

"Not just Clay," Annie replied, and forced a smile as she gave Rachel's pigtail a playful tug. "All of you."

"What?" Rachel demanded to know, her eyes growing bright with excitement.

"Can't tell. It's a surprise."

Tara pulled her head from inside the refrigerator and eyed Annie suspiciously. "What kind of surprise?"

"You'll see," Annie replied, smiling secretively.

Jase stepped outside the barn, wiping his hands on a rag, and looked toward the house, frowning. Clay should be home from school by now, he thought irritably. The boy had chores waiting.

Hearing a shout, then laughter, coming from the front of the house, he tossed down the rag. "If that boy's goofin' off when he's got work to do…" he muttered under his breath as he strode angrily for the house.

He rounded the corner of the front porch, then

ducked, swearing, when something struck him hard against the side of the face, knocking off his hat. He lifted his head as water ran down his face and dripped from his chin, narrowing his eyes on the four who stood frozen on the front lawn, staring at him in slack-jawed horror.

Clay immediately dropped the water balloon he held. "Uh, sorry, Dad," he said, taking a nervous step back. "It was an accident. I was aiming for Annie."

Jase lifted a hand and dragged it down his face, wiping the remaining moisture from his eyes and chin. "What the hell is going on here?"

"We're having a water-balloon fight," Rachel offered helpfully. "Me and Annie against Tara and Clay. Wanna play?"

Jase hauled in a breath, his chest swelling with rage as he turned his gaze on Annie. "A water-balloon fight?" he repeated. "You're having a water-balloon fight when you know damn good and well there's work to be done?"

Annie wasn't quite sure what made her do it, but as she watched Jase's face redden, saw the angry tick of a muscle on his jaw, she reared back and threw the balloon she held as hard as she could. It smacked against Jase's chest with a wet plop, exploding and shooting water up over his face and down the front of his shirt.

His eyes widened in surprise, then narrowed dangerously. "You're going to be sorry you did that," he warned as he took a threatening step toward her.

Annie thrust out a hand as if to stop him. "It's just a game, Jase," she said, laughing nervously. When he kept coming, she turned and ran.

He dived, catching her around the knees and taking her to the ground.

"I'll help you, Annie!" Rachel hollered.

Annie rolled to her back beneath Jase, her chest heaving, her heart pounding against her ribs. "It's just a game," she said again, then widened her eyes in horror when she saw Rachel lift a balloon above her daddy's head. "Rachel! No! Don't—"

But the warning came too late. The balloon split open upon impact, showering water over Jase's head and drenching his shirt.

But Jase never once moved his gaze from Annie's.

She stared up at him, her chest heaving, slowly becoming aware of the heat in his eyes, the desperate squeeze of his knees against her hips, the trembling in the hands that held her shoulders to the ground. She watched his gray eyes turn smoky, watched his gaze slide to her mouth...and had to swallow back the need-filled groan that rose to her throat.

Slowly he brought his gaze back to hers. Keeping one hand pressed against her shoulder, he lifted the other hand. "Rachel, get Daddy a balloon."

Annie's mouth sagged open. "You wouldn't dare," she cried, then shrieked and tried to wriggle from beneath him as he took the balloon Rachel passed to him and held it over her head. With a slow, smug smile spreading across his face, he squeezed his fingers around the balloon, successfully bursting it and drenching Annie's face with water.

She sputtered, laughing, trying to keep the water out of her mouth. "Unfair!" she cried.

"Unfair?" he repeated, then held out his hand again. "Tara? Give me your balloon."

Tara glanced nervously at Annie, then reluctantly dropped the balloon she held into her father's waiting hand. He rocked back on Annie's stomach and held the balloon up, cradling it between his palms.

"Don't," she begged, still laughing. "Please."

"But I thought you liked playing games?"

"I do!" she insisted, then shrieked, when he popped the balloon and water rained down over her face a second time.

"Are you kids just going to stand there?" Annie cried. "Help me out here!"

Though Clay and Tara hesitated, Rachel didn't. She grabbed a balloon from the laundry basket filled with water bombs, then leaped on her daddy's back and smashed it over his head. With a low growl, he raised his arms, wrapped them around her from behind and dragged her over his head, flipping her to the ground.

Squealing in gleeful delight, Rachel tried to scoot away, but Jase quickly shifted off Annie and grabbed her by the ankle. "Traitor," he growled, before Rachel could escape. "You know what happens to traitors, don't you?"

"No, Daddy, please!" she squealed, laughing.

Out of the corner of her eye, Annie saw Clay stealthily approaching, both hands filled with water bombs. Not at all sure how this would turn out, she pushed to a sitting position and watched in silent wonder as Clay dumped the balloons over his father's head.

A split second later, Clay was on the ground, Rachel was up and scampering away, and Tara was leaping onto her father's back, her arms wound around his neck, squealing and laughing while Jase wrestled with Clay. Rachel skipped around the pile of humans, cheerfully rooting for her brother, then her father, her loyalties switching to whoever seemed to have the upper hand at the moment.

An incredulous smile spread across Annie's face. He's playing, she thought, almost giddy at the thought. Jase Rawley is actually playing with his children.

Awareness hummed in the kitchen like something alive, all but crackled and snapped each time Annie and Jase passed by each other as he helped her put dinner on the table. Flanked by the children as they ate their meal, their gazes would meet and instantly lock, heat pulsing between them until one or the other would find the strength to look away.

Sure that she would die from the need that swirled inside her, Annie prodded the children through completing their homework assignments, supervised Rachel's bath and shampooed the child's hair, then finally escaped to her room after seeing the three off to bed.

Hours later, unable to sleep, she prowled her bedroom, every nerve in her body attuned to the man who slept in the room below hers, wondering if he would come to her, telling herself that she couldn't possibly go to him. Not after he'd told her that he wouldn't make the mistake of sleeping with her again.

Determined to take her mind off Jase, she wandered her room, rearranging the knickknacks scattered along the top of the dresser and running her palm over the cool iron rungs of her bed's footboard. When she'd first moved in with the Rawleys, she'd promised herself that she wouldn't allow herself to grow attached to this room, with its quaint iron bed and mishmash of antique furnishings. She'd also promised herself that she wouldn't allow herself to grow attached to the family she had been hired to take care of. The lesson not to form attachments had been learned long ago when she'd discovered that attachments, like promises, were meant to be broken.

She sighed and turned to the window where moonlight spilled between delicate lace panels and pooled on the wide pine planks of the floor, a circle of silver. Yes, she'd promised herself she wouldn't become attached to this house or the family who lived here, but she realized now how foolish she'd been in thinking that she could keep that promise.

She loved this room, this house and the family who inhabited it. And yes, she thought, feeling her heart constrict as she was forced to acknowledge her feelings for the man who stood at the head of it all.

She loved Jase.

Thankfully she wasn't foolish enough to believe he'd ever be able to return her love. And, though she accepted that reality, she knew that when it came time for her to go, she'd leave behind a large part of her heart. Her eyes filling with tears, she stared out at the dark landscape, wondering how many more pieces of her heart she could afford to lose, before there was nothing left to sustain her.

The thought was fleeting, much too depressing to even consider, and she turned from the window to escape it.

Pensive now, she crossed to the hallway and the stairway beyond. Keeping her tread light to avoid waking the children, she headed downstairs and out the front door. She stepped out onto the porch and to its edge, hugging her arms beneath her breasts as she drew in a deep breath of the cool night air.

Though she was dressed for bed, she wandered out into the yard, pleasure swelling inside her as she remembered the war fought on the front lawn earlier in the day. Though she hadn't planned the water-balloon fight as a means to get Jase to interact with his children, she certainly didn't mind that things had turned out the way they had. Seeing him play with his children had warmed her heart and given her hope for him and his family.

It had also eased her anger with him and left her with a keen awareness of him that seemed determined to keep her awake all night.

Sighing, she glanced back toward the house and to Jase's bedroom window, the room dark beyond the drapes that fluttered at the breeze's gentle teasing. Remembering the night before when she'd slept there in his arms, she wondered if he'd welcome her into his bed again if she were to find the courage to go to him.

She wouldn't go to him, though, she told herself firmly and turned for the barn, and she wouldn't push. If Jase wanted her, he would have to seek her out. For now, it was enough that he was interacting with his children.

Or so she told herself as she climbed the ladder to the loft for a moonlight visit with the cat and her baby kittens. Walking quietly through the tall stacks of hay, she made her way to the far corner where the mama and her kittens had made their home.

She sank down to the loft floor near the animals, gathering her gown over her folded legs. Leaning forward, she whispered, ''Hi, Mama Cat. Will you let me hold one of your babies?'' Keeping a watchful eye on the protective mother, she eased a kitten from the animal's side and drew it to her breast, cooing softly. She nuzzled her cheek against the kitten's soft fur. ''Hi, baby,'' she murmured. She held the kitten up to the moonlight that filtered through the high window and smiled as the animal opened its mouth and mewled softly, exposing a pink tongue and tiny, white teeth.

''Aren't you just the cutest little thing?'' she said, admiring its tabby stripes.

''That cute little thing will probably give you ringworm.''

Annie snatched the kitten to her chest and whipped her head around to find Jase stretched out on his side on a blanket spread over a long row of hay bales behind her, watching. Surprised to discover that he wasn't asleep in bed, as she'd thought, she asked, ''What are you doing out here?''

He rolled to a sitting position and lifted a shoulder. ''Couldn't sleep.''

Biting back a smile, she returned the kitten to its mother, then rose. ''Couldn't stand it, could you?''

He looked up at her as she crossed to him. ''Couldn't stand what?''

''Thinking about the mama cat and worrying about whether she'd be able to leave her babies long enough to find food for herself.''

He frowned and dropped his hands down to curl his fingers around the edge of the bale he sat on.

"Never gave that feline another thought after the day I first saw you taking pictures of her and her babies."

"Oh, really?" Annie said, and glanced pointedly at the bowls filled with fresh water and food.

She laughed when Jase's cheeks reddened. She draped an arm along his shoulders as she sat down next to him. "Like I said, Rawley, you're nothing but a big teddy bear."

"Yeah," he muttered. "You just keep thinking that."

She dropped an impulsive kiss on his cheek before tipping her forehead to rest against his. "Don't worry," she told him. "I will."

She felt the sigh that moved through him and the tension that slowly melted from his shoulders.

"Thanks for...well, you know," he said self-consciously.

"What?" she asked, deciding that it would make him stronger to admit what he was grateful for.

He angled his head to frown at her. "For nearly drowning me," he growled, then shoved her down on the hay.

She laughed as he stretched out over her, holding himself above her by propping a hand against the hay on either side of her face. "My, my, my," she said as she reached up with both hands to brush his hair back from his forehead. "What is all this about?"

He lowered his groin to hers, showing her. "You're lucky I was able to restrain myself earlier. If the kids hadn't been there this afternoon, I'd have taken you right there on the ground and out in broad daylight."

Shivering deliciously at the thought, she dragged her hands down his back, thrilling at the hard pads of muscle she encountered. "Seems as if I remember you saying something about this being a mistake."

He lowered himself more, slowly flattening her breasts beneath his chest as he gave her his full weight. "And nothing's changed my mind." He dipped his head down and nipped at her lower lip. "You're trouble," he murmured as he swept his mouth across hers. "Trouble with a capital T. I knew it from the first day I laid eyes on you."

"Really? So what are you doing here with me now?"

He pushed his hips more firmly against hers. "You have to ask?"

She laughed and cupped his hips, holding him against her. "Just remember. You started this. Not me."

"No. This is all your fault."

"Mine! What did I do?"

"Breathing. Existing. Seems that's all it takes."

He rolled to his back and hauled her over him. He dug his hands through her hair, his mouth seeking and finding hers in the dim moonlight. She tasted the hunger in him, felt the desperation in the hands that moved to roam her back, need in the thick column of flesh that lengthened and grew hard between them. She gloried in every touch of his hands on her, every groan that rumbled low in his throat, the heat that threatened to smother.

"You taste like sunshine," he murmured, nibbling at her lips.

"And what does sunshine taste like?"

"Golden. Warm." He swept her hair back from her face and held it against her head as he lifted his face for another taste. "And honey," he added, testing the flavor on his lips. "Sunshine and honey."

She laughed self-consciously and pressed a finger against his bottom lip. "You make me sound like something you'd order from a menu."

His gaze on hers, he caught her finger and drew it into his mouth, closing his lips around it. Heat shot through her bloodstream when he began to suckle, stealing her breath. He smiled smugly, obviously aware of the effect he had on her, and drew her finger from his mouth. He placed her hand on his chest.

She felt his heart's wild pounding beneath her palm, watched the smug smile melt slowly from his face, the heat darken his gray eyes to midnight.

"I want you," he whispered, his voice husky with need. "Even when we're apart, you're in my head, driving me crazy. I want you in spite of the fact that I know I shouldn't. I want you," he said more emphatically. "Right now."

Even as he made his intentions known, he was reaching for the snap of his jeans and ripping the fly open. Within seconds the jeans were sailing across the loft and she was beneath him, naked, her nightgown following the path of his jeans. He tore the familiar gold packet open and sheathed his sex, then, with his gaze on hers, positioned himself over her. Holding himself aloft with hands braced at either side of her head, he swooped his head down, caught a budded nipple between his teeth, then slowly drew her into his mouth as he pushed inside her.

She arched, gasping, as twin points of desire shot through her, slamming together low in her belly and ricocheting out to every extremity, leaving her weak.

Before she had a chance to recover, he was riding her, each thrust of his hips driving his sex deeper and deeper inside her.

Heat. It filled the loft, pressed down on her from every direction, slicked her skin with perspiration and sucked the oxygen from the air, making it difficult to breathe. Once her ally, heat became her tormentor, a wild, raging beast that roared its way through her, demanding release. She couldn't move or think for its mad pacing, only feel...and the hands that moved over her, seeking and finding her most sensitive spots, fanned the flames even higher. She felt shattered, fragmented, disoriented, lost in a sea of constantly churning sensations. She was desperate for something to cling to, to center herself with, a release that remained stubbornly out of reach.

Blindly, she grabbed for Jase, filling her hands with his hair, and drew his face down to hers. Before she could voice her need for him, beg him to take her, he closed his mouth over hers, swallowing her whimpered pleas. His tongue swept over hers, then stabbed deeply, matching the rhythm and intensity of his sex as he thrust wildly again and again and again.

A tidal wave of pleasure crashed over her, pummeling her senses and forcing the breath from her lungs. She tore her mouth from his with a startled cry and arched instinctively against him, her back bowing, her fingers digging into his scalp as the wave crested, flooding her body with sensation. Slowly, the tension ebbed from her limbs and her hands slipped to his back, and she soothed him while he trembled with his own release.

He drew in one last, deep shuddering breath, then

rolled to his side and gathered her into his arms and to his heart. Tucking her head beneath his chin, he pressed his lips against her hair. "You okay?" he whispered.

"Yes." She lifted her head to look up at him. "Are you?"

Jase stared down at her and smiled softly. "I'm with you, aren't I?"

Seven

If Annie had thought she'd known happiness before, she was mistaken. *This* was happiness, she decided as she flipped pancakes on the griddle. This irrepressible giddiness that seemed to bloom out of nowhere each time she thought of Jase, leaving her feeling buoyant and refreshed in spite of the little sleep she'd received the night before. Just thinking about the night of love-making in the loft and the hours spent cuddled against Jase's side on a bed of sweet-smelling hay made her sigh in contentment as she scooped golden pancakes onto a plate.

She felt a strong set of arms slip around her from behind and she melted back against a wide expanse of chest and muscled thighs.

"Good mornin'," Jase murmured against her ear as he closed his hands over her breasts.

"Good morning." Smiling, she angled her head for his kiss.

His lips were warm and achingly familiar, his freshly showered scent and his minty toothpaste taste as arousing as the hands that teased her nipples to attention.

"Kids up yet?" he asked huskily.

"Mmm-hmm," she murmured, closing her eyes against the heat that suddenly burned behind them. "They're getting dressed for school."

"After they leave, how about riding along with me while I check on the cattle?"

"On horseback?" she asked, flipping her eyes open to meet his gaze.

"We could, but I was thinking more along the lines of taking the truck."

"Oh," she said, unable to disguise her relief. "Sure. That sounds great."

Chuckling, he gave her breasts a squeeze before releasing her and taking a step back. "You don't like to ride horses?"

Feeling a little unsteady without his body to support her, she braced a hand against the stove as she began to transfer pancakes onto the plate again. "I wouldn't know. I've never ridden one."

"We'll have to fix that. But not today," he assured her when she whipped her head around to stare at him in alarm. He scooped his hat from the countertop. "You might want to pack us a lunch," he suggested. "And throw in a blanket, while you're at it." He shot her a wink as he headed out the back door. "My back's still itching from that hay last night."

Chuckling, she picked up the platter and turned.

She jerked to a stop, her eyes widening in surprise when she saw Tara standing in the doorway that led to the hall. Quickly regaining her composure, she moved on to the table. "Good morning, Tara," she said in what she hoped sounded like a normal voice. "You startled me. I didn't hear you come downstairs."

"'Morning," Tara replied, eyeing Annie suspiciously as she crossed to the table and sat down. "What did Dad mean when he said that about hay scratching his back?"

Annie prayed that the embarrassing heat she felt crawling up her neck didn't make it to her face before she turned away. "Your father couldn't sleep last night so he went out to the barn and slept in the hayloft."

"Dad slept in the loft?"

Annie glanced up to see that Clay had stepped into the kitchen, catching the end of her and Tara's conversation. "Yes," she replied. "He couldn't sleep, so he went to the barn and slept in the loft." It wasn't a lie, she told herself. Jase *had* said he'd gone to the loft because he couldn't sleep.

"That's weird," Clay said as he took his seat at the table.

"What's weird?" Rachel asked as she skipped into the kitchen.

Annie rolled her eyes, wondering how many times she would have to tell the story. Tara saved her the trouble of repeating the lie yet again.

"Dad couldn't sleep last night," the teenager told her younger sister, "so he went out to the barn and slept in the loft."

"Oh." Rachel glanced over at Annie as she climbed onto her chair at the table. "Can I sleep in the hayloft tonight?"

Annie sputtered a laugh. "No, I don't think so."

"Why not?" Rachel complained. "Daddy did."

"Yes," Annie replied patiently. "But he's an adult and knows how to take care of himself."

Rachel pushed her mouth into a pout. "I'm big, too, and I know how to take care of myself."

"Yeah, right," Clay replied dryly. "First time a coyote howled you'd be hightailing it to the house and screaming bloody murder."

"Would not," Rachel argued.

"Would, too," Clay and Tara said in unison.

And for once Annie didn't even attempt to put a stop to their innocent bickering. She was much too relieved that the focus of the conversation had turned away from Jase's—and her—night in the loft.

Sunlight filtered by the tree's canopy of leaves warmed Jase's face. The remainder of his body's warmth could only be attributed to the woman snuggled up against him. Shifting carefully, he rolled from his back and to his side, keeping his gaze on Annie's sleep-relaxed face. With the smattering of freckles high on her cheeks and on her turned-up nose, *cute* was probably a much better description of her, but he found the word *beautiful* stubbornly fixed in his mind.

She is beautiful, he argued silently. At least she was to him. And not just physically. It was her heart, her generosity, her goodness that made her so attractive. That, coupled with a sunshiny disposition and an innate sexiness that most women would pay good money to possess, made Annie a woman damn hard to resist.

And why should he try to resist her? he asked himself. He'd already tried and failed more times than he liked to think about. Besides, he'd laid out the ground rules from the get-go. A physical relationship. That was all he was interested in, and she hadn't seemed to have a problem with the restrictions he'd placed on their relationship. So why did he feel this niggling of concern now?

Because it isn't just physical anymore, you lunkhead. You care for her.

He tensed at his conscience's blunt prodding, then heaved a long, uneasy breath, knowing it was true. He did care for Annie. And if he wasn't careful, he could grow to more than just care for her. He could fall in love with her. It would be easy enough to do. She was so open and honest and warm and loving. And his kids seemed to idolize her. Even Tara, the hardest nut of the three to crack, seemed to genuinely like Annie.

Even as he thought this, Annie sighed in her sleep and snuggled closer to his chest, threading her fingers through the dark hair that curled there. Without thinking, he swept her hair back from her face and laid his palm against her cheek. A soft, sleepy smile curved her lips and she sighed again, her breath blowing warm against his chest, before she turned her lips against his chest and pressed a kiss over his heart.

Yeah, he thought, feeling the fear knotting in his gut even as desire tightened his groin.

If he wasn't careful, he could definitely fall in love with Annie.

* * *

Jase hated attending school events. Not because he felt guilty about all the work he was leaving undone on the ranch, but because his skin all but crawled at the curious looks his appearance at the events never failed to draw.

It had started years before when he'd taken over guardianship of his sister Penny, and a sense of obligation had forced him to attend the school events she participated in. People had stared at him then, some with pity, others with admiration for the task he'd taken on. But *why* they stared didn't matter to him. It was finding himself the focus of so much attention that had always bothered him, and that was the reason he usually found an excuse to avoid these functions, even when they included his own three kids.

But on this particular night Annie had refused to listen to any of his excuses and had bulldozed him into attending the Spring Fling at Rachel's elementary school.

Now he wished he'd stuck to his guns and stayed at home.

The surreptitious glances cast his way were beginning to get on his nerves. He wondered if these people didn't have anything more exciting to reflect on other than the activities in Jase Rawley's life. A couple of the single mothers who had, after his wife's death, gone out of their way to let him know that they were available if he should ever feel the need of female companionship, were busy eyeing him and Annie, as if they somehow knew their relationship was more than just that of employer and nanny. Others still looked at him with pity for the tragedies he'd suffered in his life—first the loss of his parents, then that of his wife. He figured he should be glad it was pity he recognized in a few of the glances cast his way, rather than the suspicious and jealous looks the single mothers were singeing him with.

But he quickly realized he wasn't the only one in the gymnasium who was drawing a few stares. Annie commanded a few of her own. Several of the men were eyeing her hungrily, if covertly, which irritated the hell out of Jase. He supposed he could have suggested that Annie wear something more appropriate for the Spring Fling, something that didn't draw quite so much attention her way. The yellow sundress she'd chosen to wear, with its thin spaghetti straps and flared, short skirt, begged every man in the room to take a second glance at all that smooth bare skin, the length of well-curved legs that the short skirt revealed.

Irritated by the men's admiring glances, he placed a hand low on Annie's back and hustled her toward the opposite side of the room and away from curious eyes.

"What are you doing?" she asked, having to hurry to match the length of his stride.

"I...I thought you might like some punch." He grabbed one of the filled cups positioned on the colorfully draped table and shoved it into her hand.

Annie looked up at him in surprise as she accepted the drink. "Why thank you, Jase. That's very considerate of you."

He scowled. "Yeah. Well, I can be nice when I want to be."

She sipped lemonade, smiling at him over the top of the cup. "Yes, you certainly can," she murmured suggestively, then laughed when his cheeks reddened.

"Mr. Rawley!"

Jase turned upon his hearing his name and bit back a groan when he saw Rachel's teacher bearing down on him. "Evenin', Miss Sharp," he said, giving his head a brisk nod of greeting.

"And you must be Annie." Miss Sharp grasped Annie's hand between hers and squeezed. "Rachel has told me so much about you."

Annie laughed gaily. "I hope it wasn't all bad."

"Oh, no," Miss Sharp was quick to assure her. "In fact, I expected to find a halo above your head and wings clipped to your shoulders. She simply goes on and on about how wonderful and talented you are."

Annie laughed again. "Well, I guess I've at least got Rachel fooled."

"And she's so excited about your upcoming marriage," Miss Sharp continued, beaming.

Annie's smile slowly melted. "Marriage?"

"Well, yes," Miss Sharp said, glancing uneasily toward Jase. "Oh, dear," she said, her cheeks growing pink at the thunderous look on his face. "I hope your engagement wasn't supposed to be a secret. Rachel was so excited, and she didn't mention anything about your and Mr. Rawley's plans to marry being a secret. I hope I haven't gotten the child into trouble for mentioning it. I'm sure she meant no harm."

Annie didn't dare look at Jase during the drive home. But she didn't need to look at him in order to judge his current mood. He was furious. Thus far, he'd managed to contain his anger, but she didn't suspect that he'd be able to do so for much longer. Oddly, the children seemed oblivious to their father's dark mood and were laughing and chattering in the back seat, still high from the festivities at the Spring Fling.

Once they arrived at the house, though, Jase rammed the gear shift into Park, then threw an arm along the back of the seat and turned to glare angrily at his children. Immediately the laughter in the back seat died, and the smiles melted off the children's faces.

"Rachel, did you tell your teacher that Annie and I were getting married?"

Annie turned to see tears fill Rachel's eyes.

"Y-yes, sir."

"And why would you tell her such a thing?" he asked, his voice rising measurably. "You know that it isn't true."

Rachel turned to look up at Tara. "But Tara said—"

"What did you tell her?" Jase demanded, turning his accusing gaze on his older daughter.

Tara reached for the door handle. "I told her I *thought* you and Annie liked each other, and that if you did, maybe you guys would get married."

Jase grabbed Tara's arm, preventing her from escaping the car. "We're *not* getting married. Understand? Not now, and not anytime in the future. Annie's your nanny. Period."

Tara twisted free from his grasp. "Yeah, like Annie would be stupid enough to marry *you*," she cried and bolted from the car.

A knife couldn't have penetrated Annie's heart and done any more damage. Whatever hope she had held for a more permanent relationship with Jase slipped quietly away as she stared at his shadowed profile. With tears burning her eyes, she turned to face the front and stare through the windshield.

With an uneasy glance at Annie, Clay opened the car door and caught Rachel's hand. "Come on, Sis," he murmured. "I'll help you get ready for bed."

Annie reached for her door handle, but froze when she felt Jase's hand on her arm, stopping her.

"Wait."

She dragged in a shuddery breath, blinking back tears. "What?" she asked, unable to look at him.

"You're not upset by all this, are you?"

It took all the effort she could muster, but she forced a smile as she turned to look at him. "And why would I be upset? You never promised marriage. A physical relationship, right? That's what we agreed to and that's all I expected."

Jase stood at his bedroom window, one hand braced high on the wall, looking out into the darkness, his forehead furrowed with deep grooves.

He'd hurt her. He'd hurt Annie.

He hadn't meant to, had worried from the beginning that he would if he became involved with her, had done everything in his power to avoid doing so.

But he'd hurt her anyway.

Oh, she'd put up a brave front. Even smiled when she'd insisted that she wasn't upset over his denial of Rachel's claim to her teacher that he and Annie were getting married. But he'd seen the crack in her smile, heard the tremble in her voice.

He'd hurt her.

The hell of it was, even knowing that, to his shame, he still wanted her. He wanted to slip out to the barn to see if she was in the loft with the cat and her kittens. Wanted to climb the stairs to her room and slip into bed with her.

He turned from the window, swearing under his breath as he raked his fingers through his hair. But he couldn't go to her. Couldn't hold her. Couldn't make love with her. Couldn't sleep with her cuddled against his body. Not ever again.

If he did, he'd only hurt her more.

The next few days were hell for Annie. It was difficult to maintain a smile when the children were home, present a veneer of normalcy when she was all but dying inside. More difficult still to avoid being alone with Jase, to keep from seeking him out while the children were at school. She desperately wished that she could go back to the day of the Spring Fling. If she could, this time she wouldn't force Jase to attend. If she hadn't made him go, then he would never have known that Rachel had started a rumor that he and Annie were planning to marry.

But if wishes were horses, she thought miserably, as a favorite phrase of her grandmother's came to mind, then they'd all ride.

With disappointment weighing heavily on her chest, she laid out the pictures she'd had developed, hoping to focus her thoughts away from Jase and on to potential sales she might make to magazines. In the weeks she'd worked for the Rawleys, she'd shot more than ten rolls of film; most of the children, some of the animals and plant life she'd discovered on the ranch during her wanderings.

But as she spread the prints out across the kitchen table, it was only one roll she focused on. The shots she'd taken of Jase while he'd been working with the calves in the corral.

She picked up one and sank down onto a chair, suddenly too weak to stand. He was so handsome, she thought tearfully, as she touched a finger to his face, tracing the familiar features. The high slant of cheekbones. The determined glint of flint-gray eyes. The proud lift of a square and noble chin.

She laid the picture down and selected another, this one taken in the loft when Jase had discovered her photographing the mama cat and her kittens. She'd turned the camera on him and snapped a picture of him, unaware, while he stared, mesmerized by the cat and her babies. His eyes were softer here, as were his features, reflecting the compassionate heart that he struggled so hard to hide.

Feeling the tears gathering in her throat, she glanced toward the window and the barn where Jase worked. God, she loved him, she thought, the pain of that love squeezing at an already bruised heart. But she could see the changes the revelations at the Spring Fling had left on their relationship, as well as on his relationship with his children. He was avoiding them all again. Her *and* his children. He rose before Annie even came down for the day, leaving the house and not returning sometimes until well after dark.

Though she'd planned to avoid him, he'd made the

task much too easy by first avoiding the house and her.

She'd leave.

The decision to do so was already there, in her mind and in her heart. And though it hurt to even consider leaving, she knew if she didn't, the children would lose what little part of their father they had managed to regain while Annie had been with them.

As she stood and began gathering the pictures, Annie thought perhaps she understood better Jase's sister's decision to leave the ranch. If Penny had stayed, then Jase would have continued to leave the children's raising up to her, just as he'd been willing to leave it up to Annie.

But knowing that didn't stop Annie's tears or lessen her pain.

Once again an attachment was being broken, another chunk of her heart ripped away. But this time, Annie wondered if she'd survive the loss.

From the safety and concealment of the barn, Jase watched Annie load her things into her car. She was leaving. He knew it, wanted desperately to stop her before it was too late.

But he didn't.

It was best, he told himself, as he watched her climb behind the wheel. If she stayed, it would only bring heartache to them all. To the kids. To Annie. To him. The kids would miss her, he knew. But they were young, resilient. In no time at all, she'd be just a fond memory. They'd survive the loss. They had survived others.

But would he?

Choked by tears, he watched the dust rise behind her tires as she drove down the long driveway, feeling as if his heart was being ripped right out of his chest and dragged down the road behind her. He stared until the dust had settled and her car had disappeared from sight, then dragged a hand across his eyes and headed for the house.

When he stepped into the kitchen, he saw her note on the table, propped up against the side of one of three Easter baskets filled with colorfully decorated eggs and candy. He picked up the folded note as he sank down onto his chair at the head of the table, flipped open the single sheet of paper and began to read.

Jase,

I think you know why I decided to leave, so I won't bother offering any excuses. I know it was cowardly of me to do it this way, but I honestly don't think I could bear saying goodbye to the children. I've grown to love them so much.

Since Spring Break begins at the end of school today and the children will have a week's vacation, I felt this would be the best time to make a clean break. With the twins home to look after Rachel, I'm sure that y'all can manage without me, plus it will give you a week to find a replacement. I left several casseroles in the refrigerator and instructions for reheating them, so I know you all won't starve in the interim.

Tell the children...well, tell them that I love them and that I will miss them. If they ask why I left, you can tell them that I found a teaching position in another city. It shouldn't be a lie—at least not for long, I hope. In the meantime, I've decided to do a little traveling. I might even put together a series on Texas wildflowers. Everything's in bloom now, so I should be able to find plenty to photograph.

I made Easter eggs for Rachel to hunt on Easter Sunday. They are in the largest basket. You can have Tara and Clay hide them for her. The other two baskets are for Tara and Clay. I've filled them with their favorite sweets and included pictures that I took of each of them.

Please don't think I blame you for what happened between us or think that I'm angry with you. I don't and I'm not. I knew the rules when we first began. Unfortunately, I discovered too late that my heart refuses to live by a set of predetermined rules.

I'm leaving a picture for you, as well. I took it that afternoon in the barn when you caught me photographing the mama cat and her babies. You want so badly for everyone to think you are heartless and uncaring. But look closely at the picture. I think you'll see your heart is reflected in your eyes.

Be happy, Jase. And take time for your children. They love you and they need you.

                                        Annie

Jase dropped his hand to the table, his fingers convulsing on the single sheet of paper, his sight blurred by a swirling mist of tears. Gulping, he released the note and picked up the framed picture she'd left for him and stared at his reflection. But it wasn't his own image he saw beneath the glass. It was Annie, captured by his mind's camera just as she'd looked that afternoon in the barn when they'd climbed down from the loft after photographing the cat, her face flushed with color, her green eyes bright with excitement.

She found joy in such simple things, always smiling and laughing and making those around her smile, too. And she was so generous with her time, her energy and her love, making special treats for the kids, giving them hugs when they needed them, and gentle reprimands when they needed that, too.

They were going to miss Annie.

But no more than Jase would.

Choked by the emotion that clogged his throat, he dragged the note from the table and stuffed it into his pocket as he pushed himself to his feet.

It's better this way, he told himself, as he headed for the door and the work that awaited him.

With Annie gone, he couldn't hurt her anymore.

Eight

Rachel barreled inside the barn, followed closely by the twins. Jase glanced up from his workbench, then quickly back down when he saw the smile on Rachel's face.

"Where's Annie?" she asked, hopping impatiently from one foot to the other. "She made me an Easter basket and I've got to tell her thank you."

Inhaling deeply, Jase glanced over at his daughter, then shifted his gaze higher to look at the twins who stood behind her, their expressions hesitant, almost fearful, as if they suspected Annie wasn't just missing, but gone.

He dropped his gaze. "She left."

"Left!" all three cried in unison.

"Yeah, she...she got a lead on a teaching position

that's coming open,'' he explained, taking the cowardly way out that Annie had offered him.

''But she can't leave!'' Rachel cried, her eyes already brimming with tears. ''Annie belongs to us.''

''Well, she *is* gone,'' he replied more harshly than he intended. ''So you might as well gut it up and get used to the idea.''

Tears spilled down Rachel's cheeks and she whirled and ran for the house, sobbing hysterically. Tara glared at him for a moment, then turned and ran after her little sister.

''You made her leave,'' Clay accused resentfully. ''I knew you would. I told you that if you were mean to her she wouldn't want to stay around here very long.''

''I wasn't mean to her,'' Jase argued, knowing he lied.

''Yes, you were! Annie liked it here. And she liked us, too. It's *your* fault she's gone. You always ruin everything. Everything!'' Clay yelled angrily, then spun and strode for the house.

Jase had known grief before, had experienced it at a bone-deep level that most folks his age didn't even know yet existed. But he couldn't remember ever feeling this low, this lonely.

Annie's departure had left a void in his heart and in his home. A huge vacuum that had all but sucked the life from him, his children and his house. The kids dragged around all day looking lost and forlorn, and there was a silence within his home that was almost deafening. No more wild laughter or high-pitched squeals. No more sunshiny smiles greeting him in the kitchen of a morning. No more spontaneous picnics or sensuous foot massages by the creek. No more comfort in waking to find a warm body curled against his in the night.

No more Annie.

Though he knew he should have driven into town the afternoon she left and placed an ad for a new housekeeper and nanny to take her place, Jase hadn't been able to bring himself to even attempt to write the ad, much less make the drive into town to deliver it to the newspaper. He had managed to survive the weekend. Barely. But Monday morning had dawned and he wasn't any closer to adjusting to Annie's absence than he was when he'd discovered her note on the preceding Friday. And he still hadn't made an attempt to find a replacement.

No one could replace Annie. Not in his home.

And not in his heart.

He sighed and turned from his window and crossed to his bed. Though he knew that sleep would be a long time coming, he had to at least put himself in the position to accept it if it happened to slip up on him unawares. There was work to be done. A ranch to manage. A house to run. Three kids to care for. And how could he stand up under the strain if he didn't at least try to get some rest?

He'd just dropped his head down on the pillow and stretched out his legs when his bedroom door burst open. He jackknifed to a sitting position to find Clay standing in the doorway, his eyes wild, his chest heaving.

"Come quick!" Clay gasped. "It's Tara."

Jase was on his feet and grabbing for his jeans. "What's wrong with her?"

But Clay was already running back down the hall.

With his heart in his throat, Jase followed, jerking up his zipper as he ran after his son. He bounded up the stairs and found Clay standing outside the bathroom door, staring at something on the floor inside.

Clay turned to look at Jase, his face drained of color. "I think she's dead," he said, then gulped, his eyes filling with tears.

Jase paced, holding a clinging and sobbing Rachel against his chest.

"It's okay, dumplin'," he soothed. "Tara's gonna be okay. She's gonna be okay," he repeated, and silently prayed he was right.

He glanced toward the row of curtained cubicles beyond the emergency room's glass doors and closed his eyes against the fear that gripped him, remembering Tara's ashen face, her limp and lifeless body as the ambulance attendants had wheeled the gurney she was strapped to beyond the door and into one of the cubicles, separating Jase from his daughter.

Please don't die, he prayed silently. *Oh, God, please don't let her die.*

"Dad?"

Jase opened his eyes to find Clay standing in front of him, his eyes dark with the same fear that twisted in Jase's gut.

"She's gonna make it, isn't she?" Clay asked, then gulped. "Tara's not gonna die, is she?"

Acting on instinct alone, Jase opened an arm and Clay stepped into his embrace, burying his face against his father's chest. With the arms of his youngest and his oldest wrapped around him, Jase tightened his own arms around his children, offering them the comfort he knew they needed, the same comfort he found in the arms that clung to him. ''Tara's gonna be okay,'' he assured them. ''She's gonna be okay.''

''Mr. Rawley?''

Jase jerked up his head, his heart leaping to his throat when he saw the nurse standing in the doorway. ''Yes?''

''You can see your daughter now.''

When Jase started forward, still holding Rachel on one hip and with Clay hugged against his opposite side, the nurse held up a hand. ''Just you,'' she said firmly. ''The children will need to wait here.''

Clay quickly stepped from beneath his father's arm and reached for Rachel. ''I'll watch her, Dad.''

Pride swelled in Jase's heart as he peered down at his son, realizing how much his son had grown, how much he'd matured, while Jase had been so busy ignoring his family. ''Thanks, Clay,'' he said and shifted Rachel to his son's arms. He laid a hand on Clay's shoulder and squeezed. ''I'll try to talk 'em into letting us all in,'' he promised.

With a reassuring smile for both his children, he turned and followed the nurse into the restricted area. As the nurse pushed back the curtain to the cubicle where Tara had been taken, Jase inhaled deeply, preparing himself for whatever he might have to face.

Tara lay on the gurney inside the narrow space, her eyes closed, her face as white as the pillow that cushioned her head. An IV was hooked to her wrist and tubes ran from her nose. A monitor beeped rhythmically somewhere in the room.

Jase swallowed back the fear that rose to his throat. "Is she...?"

"It was a close call," the doctor replied to the question Jase had been unable to ask, "but she's going to be fine."

The breath sagged out of Jase, leaving him weak-kneed.

"We pumped her stomach," the doctor explained, "emptying it of all the pills she took, and we're administering medication to take care of any toxins that managed to make it to her bloodstream. She'll need constant supervision for a few days, but she should be just fine."

"Thank you," Jase murmured, unable to take his eyes off Tara's pale face. With his legs trembling uncontrollably, he crossed to the gurney and took Tara's hand in his. "Tara? Baby, it's Daddy. You're gonna be all right, sweetheart. You're gonna be all right."

He felt the tears pushing at his throat, burning behind his lids, and swallowed hard as he watched his daughter's eyes blink open and slowly bring him into focus.

"Dad?"

His name was nothing more than a rusty whisper, but Jase couldn't remember ever hearing anything that sounded so good.

"Yeah, baby. It's me." He gave her hand a hard squeeze. "You gave us quite a scare, but the doctor says you're going to be fine. Just fine."

Her eyes brimmed with tears and her chin began

to quiver. "I'm sorry, Daddy. I didn't mean to scare you."

Jase dropped down on the side of the bed and smoothed the hair from her face, his heart twisting painfully in his chest. "I know you didn't, baby."

"I just miss Annie so much."

"I know, sweetheart. We all do," he admitted softly.

"I thought if I...if I was sick, she might come back and take care of me."

"Oh, baby," he murmured and leaned to press his lips against her forehead. He felt a hand slip around his neck, the tremble in the fingers that curled there, and closed his eyes against the tears that stung his eyes. "I love you, Tara," he whispered, then leaned back far enough to meet her gaze. "I love you, baby."

He saw the surprise flash in her eyes, and it was as if a huge weight lifted from his chest, freeing his heart. "I love you," he said again, a smile trembling on his lips.

"I love you, too, Daddy," she said tearfully and tugged him down to wrap both arms around his neck.

"Dad?"

Jase hefted the bale of hay high and tossed it down to the truck below. "Yeah, son?"

"Do you miss Annie?"

Jase hesitated a moment, unaccustomed to sharing his feelings, then firmed his lips, deciding it was well past time that he did. "Yeah, son, I do."

"I do, too," Clay said miserably. "And so do Rachel and Tara."

"Yeah, I know," Jase murmured.

"Do you think she would come back, if we were to ask her? Maybe you could offer her a raise or something."

Jase snorted a rueful laugh as he lifted another bale from the stack in the loft. "I doubt money would be enough inducement to get Annie ever to come back here."

"Dad?"

He tossed the bale down to the bed of the truck. "Yeah?"

"Do you miss Mom?"

Jase froze, then slowly turned to peer at his son. "Yeah. Why?"

Clay lifted a shoulder as he dragged another bale to the loft opening. "I don't know. Just curious, I guess. I miss her, too, but sometimes...well, I don't think about her as much as I used to. You know? And it makes me feel kinda guilty."

Jase pulled off his work gloves and sank down onto the bale that Clay had dragged to the opening. He patted the hay beside him, inviting his son to sit beside him. "Yeah, son. I know what you mean. But I think your mom understands. She's a part of us. Always will be. But she's gone now and she wouldn't expect us to mope around, missing her and thinking about her all the time."

"Yeah," Clay said thoughtfully. "I suppose you're right. I know I wouldn't want y'all crying and grieving all the time if I was the one who'd died."

Just the thought of losing his son had Jase reaching over and slinging an arm around Clay's shoulder and hugging him hard against his side. "I'd miss you," he said gruffly, "for a second or two," he added, hoping to tease his son from his melancholy thoughts.

Clay laughed and elbowed his dad in the ribs. "You'd better. Otherwise, I'd come back and haunt you."

Jase laughed too and scrubbed his knuckles over Clay's head before releasing him. "What's got you thinking such deep thoughts?"

Clay rolled a shoulder. "I don't know. I guess because of Annie." He glanced over at Jase. "I think she was in love with you, Dad."

Jase's heart seemed to take a dive to his boots, then jumped back up to pound furiously against his ribs. "Maybe," he said uneasily.

"More than maybe," Clay said. "I could see it in her eyes when she'd look at you. Kinda happy and wistful like."

"Now don't start imagining things that aren't true," Jase warned.

"I'm not imagining anything," Clay insisted. "Tara noticed it, too. She even thought that you were in love with Annie."

"I cared for her," Jase admitted carefully, reluctant to completely bare his soul.

"Then why'd you make her leave?" Clay asked.

Jase pushed to his feet and paced away, slapping his work gloves against his thigh. "I didn't *make* her leave. She just left."

"Because she thought you didn't want her to stay. If you'd told her you cared for her, I bet she would've stayed. I bet she'd even come back if you were to tell her now."

Jase whirled, stunned by the suggestion. ''Tell her now?''

''Yeah,'' Clay said, rising, warming to the idea. ''You could call her. Or better yet, you could go and see her. She told you where she was going, didn't she?''

''Well, no,'' Jase said slowly, his mind racing, trying to remember the details of the note Annie had left. ''Not exactly. She just said that she was going to do some traveling and take some pictures of wildflowers.''

''We could find her. I know we could. The best place in the state to view wildflowers is the Hill Country.''

''Yeah,'' Jase said, thinking of the miles of highway and country roads a search would entail. ''That it is.''

''Well, let's go!'' Clay said, slapping his dad on the back. ''We've still got a couple of days of Spring Break left, so it'll be like a family vacation. We've never taken one as far as I can remember.''

''No, we haven't,'' Jase said and began to smile. ''And it's about damn time we did,'' he added and slung an arm around Clay's shoulders and headed him for the ladder.

''How much farther, Daddy?'' Rachel whined from the back seat.

Jase glanced in the rearview mirror. ''I don't know, dumplin'.''

''I'm tired of riding in the car,'' she complained.

After two days of driving down mile after mile of roadway, stopping at motels only when it became too dark to see, so was Jase. And without so much as a single, solitary glimpse of Annie. He was about ready to call it quits.

As if sensing his readiness to admit defeat, Tara grabbed a book from the duffle bag Jase had packed for the trip. "Here, Rachel," she offered quickly. "I'll read you a story."

"Will you make all the sounds like Annie does?" Rachel asked hopefully. "And make your voice sound like all the different people?"

"Yes," Tara promised. "I'll make all the sounds."

Jase glanced in the rearview mirror and watched Tara release Rachel's seatbelt, pull her little sister onto her lap, then readjust her own seat belt to include Rachel as well.

"Once upon a time, there was a princess who lived in a castle far away—"

"That's not the way Annie sounds when she reads the story," Rachel said, frowning.

Heaving a weary sigh, Tara cleared her throat, then began again, putting an old woman's rasp in her voice.

Jase bit back a smile as he turned his gaze back to the road. He had some great kids, he told himself as he squinted his eyes against the bright sunlight. Three great kids.

Annie popped open her trunk and stored her camera equipment inside, then straightened and stretched her arms above her head to take the kinks out of her back.

She'd burned up at least six dozen rolls of film over the last five days, driven a good eight or nine hundred miles and waded through another hundred miles or more of pasture and road frontage, taking pictures of the fruits of Lady Bird Johnson's labors. Bluebonnets. Indian Blanket. Primrose. Purple Coneflower. Texas wildflowers abounded on every spot of ground and bloomed in every color of the rainbow, a rich canvas of botanical glory and history preserved and maintained thanks to the efforts of former First Lady Lady Bird Johnson.

But even the spectacular beauty of the fields of wildflowers and the peacefulness of the pastoral settings Annie had spent her time in hadn't been able to erase the memories of the Rawleys or ease the pain of leaving them.

She felt the all-too-familiar sting of tears and furiously blinked them back. She wouldn't cry any more, she told herself.

She'd already cried enough tears to keep a fleet of ships afloat.

But as she settled behind the wheel of her car, the tears remained in her eyes, blurring the last rays of sunshine as she steered her automobile from the shoulder and back onto the country road. Prepared to drive until exhaustion promised a good night's sleep, she switched the radio on to a rock station, hoping the loud music would drown out thoughts of Jase and his children.

Bone-dead tired, but unable to sleep, Jase stood at the window of the dark motel room, looking out across the parking lot and to the highway that ran in front of the motel's office. Occasionally a car would pass by and he would follow its movement until he'd determined that it wasn't Annie's.

Sighing, he braced a hand against the wall, shifting his gaze to the coils of the neon Vacancy sign, watching it flash red, then grow dark, and wondering how much more of this driving the kids could stand before they went stir crazy. At the moment, they were all asleep—Tara and Rachel in one bed, Clay in the other, sprawled across the entire bed, leaving no room for Jase. But after two days of being cooped up in a car together, all three had had about all the closeness he feared they could stand.

As he stared blindly at the Vacancy sign, an automobile pulled up beneath it, stopping in front of the motel's office. Jase straightened, sure that he recognized the car.

Couldn't be, he told himself as he waited for the car's single occupant to alight. But when the car door opened and a woman stepped out, Jase felt as if someone had whipped a length of steel around his chest and winched it up tight.

Annie.

He watched her disappear into the office, afraid to blink, afraid to move, for fear he'd lose her again. And when she returned to her car moments later, a slender strip of plastic in her hand, he turned for the door.

"Dad? Where are you going?"

Jase stopped at the sound of his son's sleepy voice and turned to peer at the shadowed bed. "Can't sleep," he said quietly, trying to keep his voice low and calm, not wanting to build false hope in his son by telling him he'd spotted Annie, for fear Annie would send him packing. "Thought I'd take a little walk. Keep an eye on your sisters for me, okay?"

"Okay," Clay mumbled. He yawned, then rolled to his side and pulled the sheet over his head.

Jase opened the door and stepped outside, closing it softly behind him. He quickly spotted Annie's car and headed for the stairs.

By the time he reached the parking lot, his breath was coming fast, his hands slick with perspiration. He stopped in the shadows and watched as she dragged an overnight bag from the back seat of her car, then waited until she approached a door on the first floor.

When she inserted the plastic card key into the slot, he stepped from the shadows. "Annie?"

She whirled, her eyes wide with fear, looking as if she were ready to bolt. "Jase?" she said, sagging when she recognized him. "What are you doing here?"

He took a step closer. "Looking for you."

Her overnight bag slipped from her fingers and clunked against the concrete walk. "For me?" She peered past him. "But...where are the children?"

He gave his head a jerk toward the stairs. "In a room upstairs. Asleep."

She whipped her gaze back to his, as if just realizing the impossibility of his knowing her location. "How did you know where to find me?"

He stuffed his hands into his pockets and rolled a shoulder. "Didn't. Been driving country roads for two days looking for you."

"But...why? Is something wrong?" she asked, taking a step toward him. "Has something happened to one of the children? Is Tara...?"

"She's okay. Or at least she is now."

He watched her face pale, her eyes darken with

fear. Realizing that he was frightening her unnecessarily, he pulled the card key from her hand. "Let's talk about this inside," he suggested and unlocked the door. He shoved it wide, then picked up her bag and stepped back, waiting for her to enter before him.

With her gaze frozen on his, she passed by him, but stopped just inside the room. "Jase. Please. You're frightening me. What's happened?"

He flipped on a light and dropped the bag inside the room before closing the door behind them. "We had a little scare several days ago," he explained, "but everything's okay now," he assured her.

"Tara?" she asked, her voice quavering.

He stuffed his hands into his pockets again and blew out a long breath, remembering that night. Tara lying on the bathroom floor. Her face white. Her lips blue. Her breathing thready, labored. The fear. The bone-chilling ride in the ambulance. "Yeah. Tara. She took a half bottle of pills."

Annie dropped her face into her open hands. "Oh, no," she moaned. When she lifted her head, her face was ravaged by guilt, her eyes gleaming with tears. "It's my fault."

"No," he said quickly and stepped to close his hands around her upper arms. "If it was anyone's fault, it was mine."

"No," she argued tearfully, shaking her head. "I shouldn't have left. I knew how fragile her emotions were, how devastating it would be for her to feel as if she were losing someone again. I should have stayed."

"Yes," he said, effectively halting her tears with

his quick agreement. "You should have stayed. But not for the reasons you think," he added quietly.

She stared at him, her chin quivering, then she firmed her lips and jerked free of his grasp. She turned away, hugging her arms beneath her breasts. "I did what I thought best at the time. What was best for us all."

"The kids didn't think so. In fact, they were plenty mad when they discovered you'd left without telling them goodbye."

She angled her head to look at him, tears flooding her eyes, her voice thick with them. "I couldn't say goodbye to them. It would have been too hard."

"Was it any easier leaving the way you did?"

She dropped her chin to her chest and the tears slipped down her cheeks and dripped off her chin. "No," she murmured miserably. "I miss them."

"And they miss you."

She covered her face with her hands. "Jase, please," she begged pitifully. "Don't do this."

"Do what?" he asked in confusion. "All I said was that the kids miss you."

She jerked her hands from her face. "I can't go back," she cried. "I won't."

"Annie—"

She took a step away from him, pushing out a hand to stop him. "No, please," she said, sobbing now. "Just go. Please. Just go."

He stared at her, wanting to argue, to take her in his arms and comfort her, to tell her he loved her, to coax and cajole until she agreed to come home with him...but found he couldn't. Not when confronted with her tears and knowing he'd caused them. Not when faced with the dark circles that lay like bruises beneath her eyes and realizing that she hadn't slept any better than he had since they'd been apart.

Not when he realized how much pain just seeing him and talking to him again caused her.

Not when reminded of how much he'd already hurt her.

Not when he feared that in her present exhausted and emotional state, she might refuse him.

"Okay," he murmured reluctantly and backed toward the door. "I'm going. But we're heading home tomorrow. If you want to come with us, you'd be welcome." He opened the door, then glanced back. "If you need me," he added quietly. "Or feel the need to talk. I'm here. Room 216 at the top of the stairs."

Nine

It took hours for Annie to finally fall asleep. And when she did sleep, she did so fitfully. After Jase had left, she'd considered climbing right back into her car and driving away, fearing that she might accidentally bump into one of the children the next morning when she checked out. Or, worse, give in to temptation and climb the stairs to room 216.

But exhaustion had kept her from leaving, and fear had kept her from going to Jase.

She knew she'd done the right thing in leaving the ranch. Remaining in Jase's home when there was no hope of a future with him, other than as his employee, was too painful to even think about.

But, oh, the children.

It had been so difficult for her to leave them, even though she'd known they were better off without her.

If she'd stayed, Jase would have continued to ignore them, just as he had for years.

And now, because they'd tracked her down, and Jase had invited her to return to the ranch, she felt as if she was being forced to leave them all over again. His offer to return to the ranch with them had been tempting. Much too tempting, she thought, tears filling her eyes. And if he'd even hinted that *he* was the one who wanted her to return, that he cared for her, and had not hidden behind the needs of his children, she might have seriously considered returning with them.

But not once during their late-night conversation had he revealed his feelings for her. Only those of his children. Which meant nothing had changed. *Jase* hadn't changed. And if she were foolish enough to return to the ranch, Annie feared Jase would slip right back into his old ways, ignoring his children and leaving their care up to her. And the children needed their father and his time and attention so much more than they needed that of a nanny.

But, mercy, she missed them, she thought, sniffing back tears as she forced herself from the bed and into the shower. Tara. Clay. Little Rachel. She'd grown to love them all so much.

But most especially Jase.

Tara waited until she heard her father's footsteps clanking on the metal stairs outside their room, then hurried to the window and pushed back the drape an inch to peek outside. She craned her neck to watch him climb into their car. "Dad's acting weird," she said, gnawing a thumbnail.

Clay folded his hands behind his head and stretched his legs out on the bed, his gaze and his attention riveted on the TV screen. ''Dad always acts weird.''

Tara shot him a frown, then peeked through the slit in the drapes again. ''Yeah, but this is different.'' She shivered as a chill chased down her spine. ''He's acting *really* weird. Yesterday he was in a pretty good mood, but this morning he looks all depressed, like somebody died or something.''

''I wanna watch 'Scooby Doo,''' Rachel complained from the opposite bed.

Clay frowned, but punched the remote, surfing through channels until he found the cartoon show Rachel requested. ''He's probably just tired,'' he said to Tara. ''He couldn't sleep last night.''

Tara whipped her head around to peer at her brother. ''How do you know that?''

Clay lifted a shoulder and tossed down the remote, resigned to watching cartoons with Rachel. '''Cause I heard him open the door and I asked him where he was going.''

''Where'd he go?''

''For a walk.''

''In the middle of the night?''

He lifted a shoulder. ''Yeah.''

''Weird,'' Tara murmured and turned her face back to the window. She watched until her father pulled out onto the highway, started to turn away, then whipped back and shoved the drape wide. ''Clay!''

''Would you clam up? Me and Rachel are trying to watch TV.''

''Clay! Come *here!*''

Muttering under his breath, he heaved himself from the bed. "Whadda you want?" he groused.

"Look," Tara said, pointing. "Isn't that Annie's car?"

Clay frowned and moved closer to the window. His eyes widened in surprise. "It sure as heck is."

The twins turned to look each other. "Do you suppose—?" they began in unison, then tripped over each other as they both bolted for the door.

"Come on, Rachel," Tara yelled.

"I don't wanna go," Rachel whined, reluctant to leave her Saturday-morning cartoons. "I wanna watch 'Scooby Doo.'"

"Annie's here!" the twins screamed at her. "Hurry!"

Rachel rolled off the bed and to her feet, blinking twice. "Annie? Where?"

"Downstairs. Now come on!"

Annie stuffed her hair dryer into her overnight bag and zipped the lid closed. Turning, she glanced around the room, checking to make sure she hadn't left anything behind, then picked up her bag. A soft knock on the door had her shoulders sagging in frustration.

Sure that it was Jase outside, she whispered a fervent prayer. "Please don't make this any harder than it already is."

Dreading another confrontation with him, she crossed to the door, dealt with the security locks and pulled it open. She stumbled back in surprise when she saw Rachel, Tara and Clay standing on the narrow walkway. She glanced behind them, then quickly looked back at the children. "What are y'all doing here? Where is your dad?"

Rachel grinned up at Annie. "He went to get us sausage biscuits from McDonalds. Hi, Annie."

Annie lifted trembling fingers to her lips, then sank weakly to her knees and opened her arms. Rachel raced into her embrace, nearly knocking Annie over with her exuberant hug. With Rachel clinging to her neck, Annie grabbed for Tara's hand and, laughing, pulled Tara down for a hug, too. "Mercy, but it's good to see you guys," she said, sniffing back tears as she squeezed them to her. She unwound Rachel's arms from her neck and stood, smiling tearfully at Clay. "Don't I get a hug from you, too, big guy?"

His cheeks flaming in embarrassment, Clay stepped forward, gave Annie a quick hug, then stepped back and ducked his head, grinning sheepishly.

Annie placed a hand over her heart, looking at each of the children in turn. "I can't believe this," she said, then laughed. "Does your dad know you're here?"

"No," Tara replied. "And he won't believe that we found you. We've been searching for you for days."

"Days and days and days," Rachel said, rolling her eyes dramatically. Then she caught Annie's hand and beamed a smile up at her. "But we found you now, and you can come back home and live with us again."

Annie dropped to a knee in front of Rachel. "Oh, no, sweetheart, I can't."

Tears welled in Rachel's eyes. "But Daddy said."

Annie glanced up at Tara.

Tara lifted a shoulder. "Dad really did say that we were going to find you and bring you back home with us." She glanced at Clay for confirmation and he quickly nodded his head in agreement.

"But I can't!" Annie cried.

"Why not?" Clay asked.

"Kids."

At the sound of Jase's stern voice, all four turned to stare at the open doorway.

"What are y'all doing down here? I thought I told you to stay in the room?"

Rachel ran to grab Jase's hand and tug him inside. "We found Annie, Daddy! See? She's right here."

Annie slowly pushed to her feet, smoothing her palms nervously down her thighs. "Good morning, Jase."

He glanced her way, his scowl deepening, then away, and focused on the wall behind her. "'Mornin'. Sorry the kids bothered you." He put a hand on Rachel's shoulder and turned her for the door. "I'll just clear them out of your way."

"Dad, no!"

Jase shot Clay a warning look. "Come on, son. I'm sure Annie's anxious to get on the road."

"But we can't just leave, Dad!" Clay cried. "We want Annie to come back home with us."

Jase glanced at Annie. "I've already asked her and she said no."

"But did you tell her—"

"Clay," Jase warned, cutting his son off.

"But, Dad!"

Tara flopped down on the bed, stubbornly folding

her arms over her chest. "I'm not going anywhere. I'm staying right here with Annie."

Jase sucked in air through his teeth. "Tara Michelle Rawley…"

She jerked up her chin. "I'm not going, and you can't make me."

Rachel pushed out her lower lip and fisted her hands stubbornly at her hips. "And I'm not going if Tara's not going."

"Dad, if you'd just tell Annie that you love her," Clay begged.

Jase whipped his head around to silence his son with a threatening look.

Tara rose slowly from the bed. "Daddy loves Annie?"

Clay squared his shoulders, boldly meeting his father's furious glare. "Yeah, he does. He told me so himself."

Tara took a step toward her father. "And you never told her?"

Jase felt the heat climbing up his neck. "Well… no…not exactly."

"Dad!" Tara cried.

Jase glanced at Annie, saw the tears glimmering in her eyes, the tremble in her chin. "I wanted to," he said. "I really did want to."

Tara gave him a shove in Annie's direction. "Well, then do it. Tell her now!"

Jase stumbled to a stop, frowning. "It's not something a man wants to do in front of an audience."

Tara grabbed Rachel's hand and dragged her sister toward the door. "Come on, Clay," she ordered impatiently, then called over her shoulder as the three hurried out the door, "Don't worry about us, Dad. We'll be in our room watching TV. Take as long as you want. Checkout time isn't until noon."

The door slammed and the sound echoed loudly in the suddenly quiet room. Slowly Jase turned to look at Annie. "I'm sorry. That isn't exactly the way I'd hoped this would go."

Annie stared at Jase, her heart lodged firmly in her throat, not daring to hope, but helpless to do anything else. Clay had said Jase loved her. Did he? And if he did, she thought stubbornly, he was going to have to say the words himself. She'd accept nothing less from him than an all-out admission. "How what would go?" she asked, then held her breath.

"This!" he cried and tossed a hand up in the air. He turned and paced away, then whirled back around. "I'd hoped to sweeten you up a little first. With roses and chocolates. They're probably wilting and melting on the front seat of the car at this very minute." He tossed his hands up in the air again. "But who the hell could hope to pull off a romantic rendevous with three kids underfoot, messing everything up all the time?"

Annie took a step toward him, then stopped, clasping her hands together at her waist. "They're wonderful children."

Jase huffed a breath, then glanced her way and had to bite back a smile. "Yeah, they are, aren't they?"

"The best."

His smile slowly faded as he was struck again by her beauty, by the pureness and goodness of her heart. "I love you, Annie. More than I can ever begin to tell you."

She took a step toward him, then stopped, her chin trembling. "But you never told me. Last night you stood right here and never said a word about how you feel. All you said was that the children missed me."

"I know," he said miserably, wanting to go to her, but fearing he'd never get around to saying all he had to say if he dared touch her. "I wanted to. Intended to. But you were so upset after I told you about Tara. It just didn't seem like the right time."

"But what if I had left?" she cried, panicking as she realized how close she'd come to doing just that. "I considered it."

"Figured you might. That's why I sat out on the steps all night."

Her eyes widened in surprise. "You sat out on the steps all night?"

"Yeah. Planned to stop you if you tried to sneak out."

Annie felt the tears building as she saw the dark circles under his eyes, his exhaustion in the weary slump of his shoulders, proof that he'd kept a vigil all night, watching her room. She lifted her hands to press her fingers against her lips. "Oh, Jase," she murmured tearfully.

"Panicked a bit this morning when the kids woke up and wanted breakfast, because I knew there was a good chance you'd slip out while I was gone." He stuck a hand in his pocket. "So I bought myself a little insurance."

Annie's mouth dropped open when he pulled out a spark plug. "You didn't!"

Ducking his head, he said, "Yeah, I did. Couldn't take a chance on losing you again." He slipped the spark plug back in his pocket, then lifted his head to meet her gaze. "Marry me, Annie," he said softly. "Marry me and put me out of my misery."

Though stunned by his proposal, she sputtered a laugh. "Put you out of your misery? What kind of marriage proposal is *that?*"

He crossed to her and took her hands, squeezing them within his. "An honest one. I've been lost without you, Annie. Miserable. More miserable than any man has a right to be and still be alive to tell it."

Laughing, she tugged her hands from his and lifted them to his cheeks, drawing his face to hers. "Many more of these pretty words and phrases, Jase Rawley, and you're likely to sweep me right off my feet."

He slipped his hands around her waist and drew her hips to his. "I love you, Annie," he said again, then brushed his lips across hers. "I love the way you look. I love the way you smell, the way you walk. I love your heart, your hands, your feet. I could even probably grow to love that blue nail polish you favor so much."

Laughing through tears of joy, she flung her arms around his neck. "And I love you."

Groaning his relief at hearing her declare her love for him, he hugged her to him, swaying with her, his cheek pressed tightly against hers. "Marry me," he said again and drew back to meet her gaze. "Marry me and be a part of my family."

Tears slipped over her lower lashes and streamed unchecked down her cheeks. "Oh, Jase. I've always wanted a family."

He thumbed a tear from beneath her eye. "Then marry me and share mine with me."

Hiccuping a sob, she flung her arms around his neck again. "Yes, yes, a thousand times yes!"

Laughing, Jase lifted her off the floor and, hugging her against his chest, spun around and around and around. "I'll make you happy. I swear I will."

"You couldn't possibly make me any happier than I am right now."

His legs bumped against the side of the bed and he tumbled down, landing on his back on the mattress. Holding Annie against his chest, he tucked his head back to meet her gaze. Smiling, he framed her face with his hands as he thumbed tears from her cheeks. "You make me happy," he told her. "More happy than a man as mule-headed as me deserves to be."

"Oh, Jase," she murmured tearfully. She rolled from his chest to lay beside him and rested her head in the curve of his shoulder. Smiling up at him, she stretched to press a kiss against his cheek, then rubbed the tip of a finger against the spot as she settled back, doubts suddenly crowding her mind. "Do you think the children will accept me?"

He reared back to look at her in surprise. "You've got to be kidding! The kids are crazy about you."

She lowered her gaze and smoothed a hand across his chest. "I know that they accepted me as their nanny." She tipped up her face to meet his gaze again. "But what about as their mother? Not that I'd ever try to replace their real mother," she added quickly.

Chuckling, Jase gave her a reassuring squeeze. "I know you wouldn't. And the kids know that, too. They love you, Annie. Never doubt that."

Sighing her relief, she snuggled closer. "Should we go and tell them?"

He turned to his side and dipped his head to brush his lips across hers. "They're busy watching TV. Besides," he said and slipped a hand beneath her blouse. "Checkout time isn't until noon."

A shiver chased down her spine as he closed a hand over her breast. "No, it isn't, is it?" she said breathlessly.

He smiled and threw a leg over hers, drawing her closer. "Nope. And I know just how to fill those remaining hours."

*   *   *   *   *

*Be sure to look for
the next book from Peggy Moreland.
Don't miss MILLIONAIRE BOSS (SD1365),
available in May 2001 from
Silhouette Desire.*

Get ready to enter the exclusive, masculine world of the...

TEXAS Cattleman's Club

Silhouette Desire®'s powerful new miniseries features five wealthy Texas bachelors—all members of the state's most prestigious club—who set out on a mission to rescue a princess...and find true love!

TEXAS MILLIONAIRE—August 1999
by Dixie Browning (SD #1232)
CINDERELLA'S TYCOON—September 1999
by Caroline Cross (SD #1238)
BILLIONAIRE BRIDEGROOM—October 1999
by Peggy Moreland (SD #1244)
SECRET AGENT DAD—November 1999
by Metsy Hingle (SD #1250)
LONE STAR PRINCE—December 1999
by Cindy Gerard (SD #1256)

Available at your favorite retail outlet.

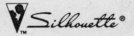

#1 *New York Times* bestselling author

NORA ROBERTS

**brings you more of the loyal and loving,
tempestuous and tantalizing Stanislaski family.**

Coming in February 2001

The Stanislaski Sisters
Natasha and Rachel

Though raised in the Old World traditions of their
family, fiery Natasha Stanislaski and cool, classy
Rachel Stanislaski are ready for a *new* world of love....

*And also available in February 2001 from
Silhouette Special Edition, the newest book in the
heartwarming Stanislaski saga*

CONSIDERING KATE

Natasha and Spencer Kimball's daughter Kate turns her
back on old dreams and returns to her hometown, where
she finds the *man* of her dreams.

Available at your favorite retail outlet.

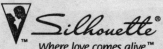

Where love comes alive™

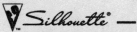

January 2001
TALL, DARK & WESTERN
#1339 by Anne Marie Winston

February 2001
THE WAY TO A RANCHER'S HEART
#1345 by Peggy Moreland

March 2001
MILLIONAIRE HUSBAND
#1352 by Leanne Banks
Million-Dollar Men

April 2001
GABRIEL'S GIFT
#1357 by Cait London
Freedom Valley

May 2001
THE TEMPTATION OF
RORY MONAHAN
#1363 by Elizabeth Bevarly

June 2001
A LADY FOR LINCOLN CADE
#1369 by BJ James
Men of Belle Terre

MAN OF THE MONTH

For twenty years Silhouette has been giving
you the ultimate in romantic reads. Come join
the celebration as some of your favorite authors
help celebrate our anniversary with the most
sensual, emotional love stories ever!

Available at your favorite retail outlet.

Silhouette®
Where love comes alive™